D1565573

BATTLE

on the Home Front

BATTLE ON THE HOME FRONT

A Navy SEAL's Mission to
Save the American Dream

Carl Higbie

Ameriman, LLC
Riverside, Connecticut
YourVirtualBookstore.com

CONTENTS

FOREWORD

In the Doha airport, I first heard Carl Higbie express his political views. A group of Navy SEALs and Navy Judge Advocate General's Corps (JAG) officers were in the midst of travel from Baghdad to Virginia Beach. After two weeks of preparing for trial and two fully contested courts-martial, two Navy SEALs finally received full acquittals in a politically charged and motivated prosecution. Time to head home stateside—the good guys just won.

The defense team and Navy SEALs involved had a flight delay that stranded them for twelve hours in Qatar's Doha airport. A few JAGs and SEALs infiltrated the duty-free store in search of booze that would go down easy with coffee and soda. Another group took over a corner of the terminal, a "Little America" in the midst of Arabs, Western ex-patriots, and world business travelers.

After an hour or two of imbibing Irish coffee and whiskey and Cokes, the issue of politics arose. I sat patiently listening to some JAGs express liberal views only to be meekly countered by some conservative JAGs and SEALs. Although counterpoints to the liberal comments surfaced in rebuttal, they lacked the zeal and confidence needed to sway the group, or for that matter, do any justice to conservative principles. That is until Carl engaged.

Hulking in the small airport chair, he leaned forward and pointed his finger at the JAG leading the liberal caucus. Carl articulated his points in a clear, concise, and commonsensical approach. His statements had force. Conviction strengthened his voice. As he steadily challenged the liberal talking points, SEALs and JAGs started to nod approvingly. Some said, "That's right," under their breath.

After several minutes, the discussion turned in to a full-out, drag-down debate between Carl and the liberal Navy JAG. They debated everything from the role of the federal government to tax reform, from the justifications for the Iraq War to the welfare state. The depth of knowledge each man possessed impressed the others and me. More impressively, I watched as Carl said what we all wanted to say but are too frequently intimidated by political correctness to express publicly.

Seeing that a deadlock was quickly approaching, and considering that we may have taken down too many of those small little bottles of Jack, I jumped in. "Guys," I said, "the bottom line is that Carl loves freedom, and the rest of you don't."

The comment got a quick laugh and allowed the group to move on to other topics, such as weather and sports.

Since that time, I have engaged Carl in political discussions. I am continually amazed at how succinctly he can express conservative views. More than anyone else I know, Carl is concerned about the direction this country is headed. He sees big government overreaching, depriving the states and citizens of the rights afforded to them in the Constitution. Worse, he sees how the mainstream media champions liberal politicians and demonizes conservatives. Additionally, Carl is pained by the politically correct policies and agenda being set forth in the United States military.

When Carl told me his plan to draft a book, I was ecstatic. After reading his work, I am impressed by his no-nonsense, commonsense approach that has the power to persuade and captivate. At times, I found myself getting frustrated by the examples of political correctness and poor decision-making he brought to light. At other points, I laughed out loud when Carl wrote about anecdotes he experienced over the last few years.

Carl has explained what is wrong with America and shown the need to restore the key pillars that make it so great: the American Dream, the belief in American exceptionalism, and the US Constitution. His viewpoint is unique in that he brings the perspective of our generation, Generation Y, coupled with what he has seen and experienced as a combat veteran and Navy SEAL.

Perhaps with this book, Carl can motivate others to make a change, get involved, and do their part in bringing this proud and resilient country to even higher levels of greatness.

GUY RESCHENTHALER
Former Navy JAG Lieutenant

PREFACE

Laying It All Out

Strap in, America! I am about to say what most of you have been thinking but are too afraid to say. Some things I have said in this book will, I'm sure, be construed as rude, prejudiced, biased, sexist, racist, and any other word you can tie to offending someone.

To set the record straight, I am intolerant—not against skin color, race, or religion, but against some beliefs, morals, and actions. I do hate people who don't offer anything when they have the ability to do so. You may think that is savage. Fine. We are still animals, no matter how civilized we think we are.

Call me crazy or a rebel; that will be taken as a compliment. Our founding fathers were called such things when they broke away from England and founded the greatest country in the world.

If you call me unreasonable, radical, or extreme, I encourage you to present another solution to prevent the almost inevitable downfall of this country.

If you call me heartless, I assure you I'm not. Talk to my family. I love my wife unequivocally and would lay my life down for her not to endure a hardship. If you happen to have a flat tire on the side of the road in a monsoon, I assure you I will be the one to stop and help you fix it.

PREFACE

I am a true, red-white-and-blue-blooded, flag-loving, meat-eating, Harley-riding, gun-owning American, who has lost his tolerance for the outrages of today's society. I love this country wholeheartedly, and am prepared to die for it. Nothing you can call me in that light will offend me, but will only strengthen my patriotism. Many of the things my opposition calls me I will take as a compliment, because their insults are, in fact, setting me apart from them and defining my very point.

ACKNOWLEDGMENTS

Special thanks for unwavering patriotism in these individuals:

Guy Reschenthaler (former Navy JAG Lieutenant). By your unwavering patriotism, moral balance, and unparalleled devotion to democracy, you provided the help and support necessary to bring this book and our fight to save America to the doorsteps of those who oppose the American dream.

Jim Lenihan (civilian attorney). Your dedication to America and knowledge of law made this possible while I served on active duty.

The men and women who have served and still serve this country. America is and always will be in your debt.

Dennis Keegan. Through your support, my fight became a reality.

ONE

My Background

Before I state my views and thoughts, I want everyone to know where I come from and the lifestyle upon which my views are based.

I grew up in an upper-class town called Greenwich in southern Connecticut. I was part of what is now known as "the boomerang generation," so named because so many of them boomeranged back home to live with their parents into adulthood. All my life I have done things a bit differently. I have stood up for what I thought was right, even against the majority. I have never much cared what people thought about my opinion or me and will, therefore, go to great lengths to make my opinions clear.

I was raised with the traditional American values as paramount. The laws of right and wrong—baptism and communion, don't live beyond your means, work hard and prosper—ruled our household. While every family has its issues, we were a fairly normal household. My two sisters—Christine, four years younger than I, and Catie, eight years younger—excelled at school and competed in a variety of sports. My mother and father both held office jobs until I started middle school, at which time my mother became a stay-at-home mom and a very politically involved person in the town. Sunday night dinners, Saturday morning cartoons, and playing in the woods were the norm on the weekends. During the week, there was the morning race prior to school and afternoon sports prior to homework. We were a well-off but nevertheless run-of-the-mill family.

From birth I was a dedicated and determined rebel, willing to do whatever was necessary to accomplish whatever I had set my mind to do. One of my earliest memories of this determination was a snowy December morning at the age of four. My father was splitting firewood for our living room fireplace, as he did every year. I was an ever-present minion, stacking wood or carrying it to the wheelbarrow, but I had not swung a splitting maul to date.

As my dad rolled a fresh-cut three-foot-diameter oak log to the splitting area, I decided I wanted to tackle this one. I asked my dad if I could do it, and he chuckled and hesitantly said yes (perhaps he thought I was joking). He made the first swing to set the wedge dead center. Then he handed me the eight-pound maul, and I began pounding. I could barely get the heavy hammer above my head, let alone assist gravity in getting it to the wedge, so it just fell under its own weight until it made the clinking contact.

My father stood there and watched for about ten minutes, seeing very little progress, before heading inside to grab some coffee and watch me through our kitchen bay window. Swing after swing, I hammered the wedge through the dense and knotted oak log for almost two hours. Finally the log split, half falling to the left and half to the right. My dad came running out laughing and told me how proud he was of me. There was still a lot of splitting to go, but I was content, so in the interest of finishing before spring, my dad and I resumed our traditional roles.

BRUNSWICK

As I attended a small private school in my hometown called Brunswick, from pre-K to sixth grade, I had a number of issues that all stemmed from a problem with authority and a don't-take-junk-from-anyone attitude. The school was a very strict and preppy environment for which I was not suited. I hated those people, who seemed to me the definition of wimpy progressives and liberals— such as people in Congress who need to shut up and put their money where their mouths are. There was really only one person with whom I got along.

Bunker came to Brunswick in second grade and is still my best friend today. Naturally, because I did not fit in and would not adhere to the preppy ways of tennis, golf, and popped-collar polo shirt cliques, I was subject to criticism among my peers. Telling the teachers brought little to no result, so by third grade I wouldn't hesitate to tell my fellow classmates what I thought about their teasing and smug jokes. Those confrontations usually led to fights, and I often got beat up because I would take on a group of four or five other kids. Somehow I was always at fault and had frequent visits to the principal's office. Since I didn't want to be there anyway, I really didn't care. I was going to defend my honor one way or another, and I had the system figured out. While violence wasn't my first option, it certainly was never ruled out as a subsequent one. The problem was that, much like a military chain of command, which I will discuss later, the way the school wanted me to solve problems was idealistic, nonconfrontational, and ultimately ineffective.

> The way the school wanted me to solve problems was idealistic, nonconfrontational, and ultimately ineffective.

If you had a problem with another student and told the teacher, the teacher would talk to the other student about it, and then you were known as a "tattletale," which at that age subjected you to even more teasing. My plan was to skip the teacher and tell the other student he had a choice: to stop or get punched in the face. The student would either stop or try to call my bluff, which, having the element of surprise, made it easy to get off a quick and devastating punch to the face before his friends jumped me, or the fight was broken up by other classmates and teachers. Not only did that kid never make fun of me again, but neither did anyone else in his clique for fear of the same fate. The problem was, since many people in the educational field are left-wing, nonconfrontational hippies who think everything can be solved by words and negotiations, this did not go well for my career at Brunswick, and I was asked to leave at the end of my sixth-grade year.

THE RECTORY

Due to my poor academic performance and stubborn attitude, I was held back at my next school and repeated sixth grade. The Rectory, a preparatory boarding school in Pomfret, Connecticut, was founded on religious values and designed to accommodate kids with "educational problems." By that point, my parents had sent me to a slew of shrinks, and I had been prescribed every medication under the sun for anything from Attention Deficit Hyperactivity Disorder (ADHD) to bipolar disorder. I had none of them—I simply hated the atmosphere into which I was forced, which was supported by my performance in classes and scenarios that I thought were worthwhile and enjoyable.

Things at the new school didn't work out well either. Why? Because I was surrounded by what seemed to me the same type of preppy, spineless wimps and self-righteous, conceited teachers as I was at my previous schools. There were only a handful of teachers at either school who genuinely seemed to care about the students' well-being. These schools all had a few things in common: they tried to take away the individualism of the child and funnel them into the robots that their Wall Street-oriented parents wanted, and they were run by the same type of anti-patriotic liberals who have sent this country into the socialist downward spiral of today. This, combined with the fact that I was an unattractive, chubby kid, who tried to be a skateboarder and played the tuba, with no chance of landing a girlfriend, made me pretty irate.

One day in woodshop class, just before Christmas vacation, I made a smart-alecky comeback to a kid two years older than I was for making fun of my Hawaiian shirt. He proceeded to beat me up; so in the interest of survival, I grabbed the closest lifesaving tool I could find and swung at him with it, sinking the medium-sized Phillips-head screwdriver into his left thigh. Needless to say, I was asked not to return to school after Christmas break.

Three Springs

At that point, my parents were freaking out, and I'm pretty sure shooting me and burying my body out back had crossed their minds, and rightfully so. Just after the New Year, I was shipped off to Three Springs, an outdoor therapeutic treatment facility in Bucksnort, Tennessee. The best way to describe this dump was "Outward Bound meets a labor camp," with campfire discussions every night about how screwed up we all were.

It was at my first campfire powwow when I realized that, though I had my issues, I was in the wrong place. The other kids in my small group were there for things like massive drug use, attempted murder of their parents, multiple suicide attempts, and court-ordered sentences after multiple arrests. I was assigned anger management and authority conflict as my issues. Later, when I voiced my opinion about how living in the woods for almost a year with a bunch of fifteen-year-old gangsters and criminals was a bit of a knee-jerk reaction by my parents, they tacked on "narcissistic behavior," as the morbidly obese on-site shrink thought I had a mind-set of being better than those people. That set me off to no end; a guy with no sense of personal discipline with regard to his own weight was telling me I had a problem.

MY NICHE

Nevertheless, I completed the program two months earlier than usual and finally got my wish of going to a mainstream public high school. Entering my freshman year a month late was a bit of an adjustment. I showed up on the football field for tryouts weighing barely 110 pounds soaking wet. I was asked if I had ever played, to which I responded, "Not really." So they told me to go stand over on the sideline until I got the gist of it.

Knowing what that meant, I walked back into the gym area where the wrestling team happened to be having preseason practice. I asked a short, bald guy yelling from the edge of the mat if I was too small. Dick Leonard, probably one of the wittiest men I would come to know, chuckled and said, "Well, you could fill one of our wimp weight classes, so jump on in."

A little annoyed, but still happy to be a part of something, I jumped in with a few guys my size, who proceeded to take me down at will and rough me up. (Fortunately for them, there were no screwdrivers around.) After about thirty exhausting minutes of round-robin takedown drills, the head coach blew the whistle, and a couple of the guys invited me to go to the weight room with them. Having a lifelong love for exercise, I happily agreed. As soon as we strolled in, I was hooked.

> I had one goal in mind, and I knew I didn't need a 4.0 grade point average to meet it. I wanted to be a Navy SEAL.

Throughout the rest of my high school career, I distinguished myself as a star wrestler, eventually winning county twice, state once, top five in New England, and becoming one of only a handful from our school ever to compete at nationals. I was a mediocre student. Not because I was stupid, but because I had one goal in mind, and I knew I didn't need a 4.0 grade point average to meet it. I wanted to be a Navy SEAL ("Sea, Air, and Land" teams).

ABILITY AND RESPONSIBILITY

At the beginning of my senior year, I was in gym class running on a treadmill when I looked at the TV and saw one of the Twin Towers on fire after one of the airplanes crashed into it. That incident reinforced for me the idea, which is often contrary to popular belief, that everyone owes a little something more to their country. Life is not just about benefiting you. Those who have the *ability* have the *responsibility*. I had been raised to believe that, unless you went to college after high school, you would not amount to anything. So despite wanting to join the service right out of high school, I was accepted to Sacred Heart University in Fairfield, Connecticut, and started in the fall of 2002. I wrestled there for my freshman year and more or less coasted through my classes. My heart was not in it. The only reason I stayed there was to wrestle, and even that wasn't fully satisfying, because I felt as if I were wasting valuable time that I could have spent doing something for my country.

My sophomore year came around, and I was even less interested. As a commuter the year before, I really hadn't made a close group of friends, except for those on the wrestling team. I was boarding that year, and I lived with a bunch of typical college kids, who played third string in some sport in high school, if that, relived it every day, and mooched off of Mommy's and Daddy's financial successes with no drive of their own. All they cared about was drinking on the weekends, "banging chicks," and wasting their parents' money. These were the guys who popped their collar, wore boat shoes every day, and thought that shaggy hair and the Dave Matthews Band were cool. Not one of the ten guys I lived with seemed as if he would ever amount to anything or, for that matter, even wanted to amount to anything, let alone serve the country that grants them the very rights they enjoy. It was during that time I realized I had to make a change. I said I would finish out the semester and then join up with the navy to become a SEAL.

Things happened a little faster than anticipated. About a week later, I got my English paper back. The topic was "Would you describe this book as good literature?" As you can probably imagine, someone like me was not going to put a lot of effort into an essay with that topic on a book that I didn't even care about.

I got a big red "F" and a "See me" at the top of the paper. After class, I stuck around and met with the teacher. He said, "Carl, you didn't answer the question at all."

I replied, "Yes, I did. You asked if I thought this was good literature, and I centered the entire essay on my not enjoying it or being able to relate to the topic, aside from thinking the book sucked." Since I had only read the CliffsNotes, I could have been wrong.

"Well, Carl, that's not what good literature means."

By that time, I was getting more and more aggravated, because I don't generally like teachers, and particularly English teachers. They usually are the sort of progressive elitists that somehow believe they are smarter than everyone else. As I clenched my teeth, I said, "Sir, I responded to what I thought was the question, and if you had a more specific idea of an answer, you should have stated that in the question."

"Carl, everyone else in the class got it right, so it is your ignorance to the question that served you wrong."

I was already angry, and that sent me over the top. "Are you freaking serious?" I said with a shocked look on my face.

He looked at me with the same I'm-smarter-than-you sneer with which he had started and said, "Maybe college isn't for you."

I sat there for a minute contemplating choking him right there in the classroom as he packed his briefcase and eventually left. I stuck the paper in my pocket and walked outside to my car just in time to see that same teacher drive by me in his pathetic little Honda Civic. As he passed, he gave me a queer, condescending smile. I only saw it for a second until the bumper sticker on the back of his car caught my eye: "Make Peace, Not War."

Enlisting

That infuriated me even more. So I got into my car and drove to the recruiting office, thinking the entire time, *does this guy even know that every day he reaps the benefits of so many fallen Americans who fought wars for him? What a coward!* I walked into the building and was instantly greeted by a marine, who wanted me to sign up with him. I walked right past him and into the navy recruiting office. There was an anxious E-6 waiting to sign me up as I sat down at his desk.

"I'm going to be a SEAL, and I need you to do all the paperwork," I said.

He laughed and quickly became serious again when he saw I was not amused. "Well, let's start some paperwork, shall we?" he said. This guy was a skinnier version of the Simpsons' character Ned Flanders in a navy uniform. I couldn't help thinking, *this guy is a member and representative of our nation's military? Lord, help us.*

We went through the preliminary paperwork, discussing my goals, logistical information, and when I wanted to leave. Under the impression I was leaving that day, I told him that I just needed to run home to get a few things, and I was ready to leave. He chuckled and told me the soonest I could go to boot camp was April of the following year.

I replied, "Are you serious? That's seven months away. You're telling me that we just declared a global war on terrorism, and you can't get me into the military sooner than April? Wow! The government is inefficient."

With a blank look on his face, he just buried his face in some papers and said, "Yup."

It took about an hour to do all the paperwork. He then asked me if I had told my parents. Of course I had mentioned that I was going to be a SEAL one day, but I had not told them about my immediate decision. He told me he would drive me home to talk to them about it. We got in the car and drove the twenty-five minutes back to Greenwich to my parents' house.

I walked in the door escorted by the recruiter and saw my mother standing there with the most confused look on her face. She asked, "Buddy, what is going on?"

I looked at her with a slight smile and said, "Done with school, going to be a SEAL now."

There was a long pause as my mother rifled through the thoughts in her head about how she wanted to freak out at me. "We'll talk about this later, Bud."

"Nothing to talk about, Mom. I've already signed up, and I've made my decision."

Her eyes watered up as she left the room. I told the recruiter that I was all set, and I would deal with her later. That night we drove up to Military Entrance Processing Station (MEPS), some processing facility in southern Massachusetts. I spent the night there, and the next morning I was subjected to the standard testing and screening. I took medical tests, written tests and, of course, endorsed the contract where you sign over your soul. After all was complete, the same recruiter was there to pick me up and bring me back home. We made a brief stop at Sacred Heart to grab all my stuff from my dorm room, and he helped me load my car. Every one of the guys I lived with thought I was insane for leaving college to join the military. They were too self-absorbed to think about doing anything that didn't benefit them.

As I walked in the door that evening at my parents' house, I could feel the tension. My dad was so upset that I was not going to finish the semester that they had just paid for in full that he had taken the day off from work in the city and waited for my arrival home. Here it comes, I thought. Before unpacking my belongings, I sat down to dinner. It was quiet at first, and then my dad said, "Bud, I really wish you would at least finish this year at college."

"Dad, I didn't even want to go to college in the first place, but I did it because I thought it was what you wanted. It's just not for me, and I feel I have a lot more to offer as a SEAL than as a college student."

After some more bickering, I put my fork down, said good night, and went to my room. No one bothered me the rest of the night.

> If my parents didn't hate me before, then they are definitely going to hate me now.

The next day, out of anger, I was speeding on wet roads and totaled my parents' '99 Ford Explorer by running right into a tree. I was so hacked off at myself, and all I could think was, *if my parents didn't hate me before, then they are definitely going to hate me now.*

INTERIM DUTY

Being out of school, having no job, and with nothing really planned for the next seven months left me feeling pretty worthless. Thankfully, I had a close friend who hooked me up with a sweet '89 VW station wagon. From his house I went right to see another friend named Rick, who owned a boatyard down the street, and I asked for a job until I shipped off to the navy. Rick introduced me to another guy named Jan Hansen, who at the time was renting a corner of the boatyard.

Though Jan was about twenty years older than I, we hit it off pretty well. He is one of the most honest, hardworking, and genuine people I have met to date. He owned and still operates a small marine construction company that did dock building, renovation, and salvage work in the area. Being paid pretty well, doing a lot of manual labor, and being outside, I was very happy with that job until I shipped out to boot camp. Also, hearing that I was home, my high school wrestling coach and longtime role model, Brad Wallace, asked me if I wanted to be the assistant coach in the evenings. Of course, as a former LL (the largest high school division) state and two-time county champ, I was more than happy to accept.

For the next six months, I worked hard from 5:00 a.m. to 2:00 p.m. on the barge with "Jan Han" as I called him. Then I spent 2:30 to 6:00 p.m. with Brad at wrestling practice, Monday through Friday. Usually Jan and I worked weekends, too, for a few hours a day, just to catch up with the ever-compounding workload he had.

I had also been introduced to a local SEAL reservist. He ran a program that helped get us ready for the initial screening test prior to the severe program we were volunteering for called Basic Underwater Demolition SEAL training (BUD/S), the preliminary seven-month screening to becoming a SEAL. Soon after showing up at the first training session of his prep course, I was told that I would definitely not make it through the training and would not receive his recommendation at BUD/S. "Who cares?" came to mind. I was still going. As the end of March came around, I started getting things ready to leave. I told Jan that I was finished, said my good-byes, and tied up loose ends before I officially entered the navy. Of course, I would never have left without a massive going-away party, which I paid for the next morning when I woke up in an interesting setting and with a huge hangover.

ANCHORS AWEIGH!

It was April 4, 2004, and while waiting in my parents' kitchen for the recruiter to arrive and take me away, my mother asked me, "Bud, are there any more guns, knives, explosives, or anything else questionably legal in the house?"

I ran upstairs to double-check any number of my secret caches and found one more two-pound Pyrodex and ammonium nitrate pipe bomb with a thirty-second fuse on it. I came trotting down the stairs with it in my hand, intending to detonate it in the back yard before I left. By that time, the recruiter had arrived and was explaining to my parents how I was making an honorable decision and blah, blah, blah, the usual sales talk they give to help themselves sleep at night after dishing out all the lies they tell you to get you to join. My entrance into the room with the equivalent of a little over a pound of TNT was a little shocking to the recruiter but was déjà vu to my parents. My mom, despite years of my antics, proceeded to tell me that we should give it to the police, and they would take care of it. I laughed, as I knew I had them in a checkmate situation, and said, "Mom, right now the best thing for all of us is for me to light this fuse and pretend it never happened—what do you say?"

"Okay, Bud, but I hope it's not too loud," said my dad reluctantly.

I grabbed a lighter and walked outside, instructing everyone to stay inside. I lit it and threw it over the stone wall about forty yards from the back of the house. That was not my first rodeo, and I ran inside quickly. Thirty seconds or so of silence went by, which was broken by an earth-rattling *bang!* that shook the pictures on the wall and launched nearly a cubic yard of dirt over two hundred feet in the air.

I smiled and looked at the recruiter, who had nearly wet his pants, and said, "Okay, ready when you are."

I bid my last good-byes to my family and was off. As I drove down the driveway, I shed a tear. Not really sure what I was upset about, I turned around and looked at the recruiter just in time for him to tell me, "I think you'll fit in just fine at BUD/S."

Boot Camp

Boot camp was a miserable experience and taught me nothing about anything useful except for the ranking system in the navy and folding my clothes.

Immediately after graduating from boot camp, I was off to "A" school. Prior to going to BUD/S, everyone in the navy had to pick a job, because of the high attrition rate from the training. That way, if you quit or fail, the navy can put you right to work in the fleet. I picked Store Keeper (SK) for a rate or job title, because it was the shortest school available, and it got me to BUD/S the fastest. That was another month of my life I will never get back. It was truly amazing that those fat slobs at the schoolhouse, who sat behind desks and ordered whatever needed to be ordered, had the view that they were the best the navy had to offer.

For example, every morning we had group workouts prior to classes, which usually consisted of a total of five or ten sets of ten push-ups mixed with an equal amount of sit-ups and jumping jacks, all followed by no more than a two-mile run at just over a walking pace. The same instructor always led these PTs, as we called them, while the others walked around hassling the class because they were too fat or out of shape to complete it themselves.

On one of those runs, I spoke up and asked if I could do PT on my own, because I was in training for BUD/S, and that program was hurting my training. That was met with serious criticism. One of the instructors said, "If you think you can do a better job, why don't you lead PT tomorrow morning?" Confused as to whether that was meant to be a punishment or not, I accepted. The next morning, I was amped and ready for a good workout. I kicked off the workout with a quick warm-up, followed by ten sets of progressively more intense sprints. We then broke the one-hundred-person group into five stations of push-ups, sit-ups, lunges, pull-ups, and fireman carry squats. Even before the first rotation was complete, the same instructors who gave me the task intervened. Apparently that twenty-five-minute workout was too intense for a bunch of soldiers. I was instructed to skip over to the run, which I extended to three miles at a reasonable eight-minute pace. Wrong again. Less than half a mile into the run, I was reprimanded and moved to the back of the pack, and the traditional instructor took over. My reaction was probably similar to yours as you are reading this: hooyah military, right? Finally, with the administrative boxes checked, I was off to BUD/S, but not without a quick trip home to party with the good ol' boys.

It was then August, and I had just landed in San Diego, California. I waited on the curb in my dress whites for the duty driver to pick me up and take me to the compound where I would live for the next seven months. Some guy who had previously quit showed up and told me to get in. The drive was short, but I was all too ready to begin my real journey. He walked me across the grinder where there were a number of helmets from people quitting and said, "Don't be one of those guys." I didn't say anything and continued walking to the quarterdeck. No sooner had I walked in the door than a BUD/S instructor started yelling at me to go get wet and sandy. I smiled and took off to the ocean, over the fifteen-foot-high sand berm and into the fifty-five-degree water. On the way back, I dove into the sand and rolled till I was covered head to toe. I made it back to the same instructor as fast as I could and stood at attention. I had never been so proud. Here I was, about to start the most elite military training in the world; nothing could bring me down.

> When-ever you thought it couldn't get harder, it did, over and over again.

The next seven months were about as hard and miserable as they could get. And whenever you thought it couldn't get harder, it did, over and over again. Everyone who was there for the right reasons had the same mentality; we laughed and toughed it out every day.

SEAL at Last

Graduation from BUD/S came, and everyone shipped off to jump school as the next part of the pipeline. Jump school was three weeks that could have been made into three days; leave it to the military to drag stuff out. After graduating from jump school, we started SEAL qualification training (SQT), the final step to becoming a Navy SEAL. Six more months of intensive training got us to that glorious day on September 30, 2005. Thirty of the original three hundred who had started stood there in front of the biggest flag I had ever seen, all with the same feeling of honor. Never have I been more proud. As we were individually called up to receive our trident pin from then three–star Admiral Olsen, I thought, I'm almost there. I've almost earned the right to call myself a true American patriot.

Checking into the SEAL Team, however, took me down a few notches as I began my career as a "new guy"—pretty much lower than dirt. For the next eighteen months, we had to earn our right to be called SEALs all over again. More training and tons more harassment from the seasoned veterans of the team would get us ready for what was about to be one of the most action-packed deployments spec war—meaning Special Warfare—had ever seen.

On April 5, 2007, I was getting on my first plane to go to war. I was so excited—my dream was finally here. After all the "stuff" I had been through, I was finally getting on a plane to go serve with the best warriors this world has ever seen.

Over the next few days, we got acquainted with the schedule in Baghdad, Iraq. We went out on ops (operations), or missions, frequently, but we hadn't seen too much action yet. Then one night about three weeks after arriving, it happened. That sweet sound of enemy gunfire and the snaps as the bullets whizzed past my head. I returned fire along with one of my teammates. The enemy dropped behind the wall out of our line of fire. I called our air asset above. "Delta 2, this is Echo 5. Fire mission, over."

"Echo 5, Delta 2. Send it."

"My position southwest corner of target block, marked by IR strobe, three pax on rooftop seventy-five meters west of my location, all hostile."

"Roger, searching . . . contact three hostiles seventy-five meters west your pos—contact muzzle flash, rounds coming down." There was a slight pause, and then five distinct consecutive explosions.

"Echo 5, Delta 2."

"Go ahead, Delta 2," I responded.

"Three EKIA (enemy killed in action). Follow on?"

With the biggest smile on my face, I said, "Negative follow on, Delta 2. Contact Echo 9 for further instructions."

The drive back to base was tough; I was falling asleep at the wheel after the adrenalin had worn off, but I was so proud. Sitting in my room that morning upon return, I hung an American flag on my wall. I took a step back and stared at it for a while. After more than three years of training, I had done it. I had fought for my country. I was the proudest person in the world. You could have clubbed me over the head, and I would have just stood there and stared at the flag.

> I had fought for my country. I was the proudest person in the world.

Action continued to ramp up over the course of the summer, but no one complained. We were all there for the same reason, and everyone was happy to be a part of the show.

My Goal

Now married to the most unbelievable woman in the world, and having had a chance to mature, I completed a second deployment to the Middle East and then was shifted to a training command. As the war in Iraq was dying down, and the troops were pulling out, I had the time to think a lot more about America and what it has become, and I began writing. This book is my perception of the greatest country on earth, which I see slipping away from the principles on which it was founded.

I am a true, red-white-and-blue-blooded American, not just because I was born here, but because I love this country with all my heart. I'm no different or better than anyone else out there. I set goals, and I work hard to achieve them. As I was told as a child, you can do anything you set your mind to do. I am setting my mind to get this country back on track, back to what our forefathers intended it to be. We owe it to them, our children, and ourselves. I will accomplish my goal. Failure is not an option.

TWO

America's Founding Principles

The United States, as most people know, was founded on the principles of the Judeo-Christian teachings of right and wrong. One of the driving forces behind the Revolutionary War was taxation without representation. People believed it was wrong, and they stood up against it. We defeated England and established our own nation with a constitution empowered by the people for the people—a strong foundation for a new nation that was followed by strong leaders who continued to mold this country into what, over time and built on these men's shoulders, became the greatest and most powerful nation ever. This is the land of the free because of the brave. George Washington, Thomas Jefferson, Ulysses S. Grant, and Abraham Lincoln are great American icons, and all distinguished themselves with honorable careers or events that gave them the credibility to lead. But today we have started to return to the big-government ideology from which we fought so hard to break free.

Religion

Religion offers a set of guidelines for beliefs and behaviors that lead to spiritual prosperity and the ability to live a moral life, principles on which the initial laws and standards of this country were founded. While I don't personally believe in big, organized religion, I firmly believe in Christian teachings and what religion stands for and represents. The Bible contains a set of morals we were meant follow. I have no problem with people believing in their form of organized religion; in fact, I encourage it, because faith in something breeds personal strength. Every time I go off to war, many people tell me they are praying for me. "Thank you," I say, because I genuinely believe they are giving a piece of themselves to help me. Today the liberal side of the spectrum is trying to degrade religious faith or take God and any organized religion out of this country under the guise of separation of church and state. By the way, that concept was not in any founding federal documents and was only stated in a letter to the Danbury Baptists from Thomas Jefferson in 1802. Its intent was to protect the church and religious individuals from the state to avoid sway in political matters in support of the First Amendment. The letter read as follows:

Gentlemen,

The affectionate sentiments of esteem and approbation, which you are so good as to express towards me, on behalf of the Danbury Baptist association, give me the highest satisfaction. My duties dictate a faithful and zealous pursuit of the interests of my constituents, and in proportion as they are persuaded of my fidelity to those duties, the discharge of them becomes more and more pleasing.

Believing with you that religion is a matter which lies solely between Man and his God, that he owes account to none other for his faith or his worship, that the legitimate powers of government reach actions only, and not opinions, I contemplate with sovereign reverence that act of the whole American people which declared that their legislature should "make no law respecting an establishment of religion, or prohibiting the free exercise thereof," thus building a wall of separation between Church and State.

Adhering to this expression of the supreme will of the nation in behalf of the rights of conscience, I shall see with sincere satisfaction the progress of those sentiments which tend to restore to man all his natural rights, convinced he has no natural right in opposition to his social duties.

I reciprocate your kind prayers for the protection and blessing of the common father and creator of man, and tender you for yourselves and your religious association, assurances of my high respect and esteem.

T. Jefferson
Jan. 1, 1802[1]

This was the introduction to the fiasco that has allowed people to ban crosses and other founding symbols from federally funded areas and even some private organizations. Disrespect for Christianity has even gone so far as putting a sculpture in the Smithsonian Museum depicting Jesus covered in ants. Don't forget that on our currency it says, "In God We Trust." Guess what? While it may not be your definition of God, and you may not agree with it, everyone needs to understand that there are greater forces at work than just mankind. Judgment will be passed one way or another. All people will get what they deserve eventually. Whether you believe in it or not, religion is a huge part of this country, and no one has the right to take that out of the already established and successful system. If you disagree, read the Pledge of Allegiance. You are welcome to go live in another country that shares your views.

> "If we ever forget that we're 'one nation under God,' then we will be a nation gone under."
> —RONALD REAGAN

"If we ever forget that we're 'one nation under God,' then we will be a nation gone under," said former president Ronald Reagan.[2]

Work and Responsibility

After religion, hard work and personal responsibility are exactly what made this nation great. If you look now, that's not really the case anymore. Too many people think that the government owes them something. What's more, too many people take handouts with no intention of giving back or aspiring to be anything more than a drain on society. The problem is that it has been engrained, especially in today's generation (more on that later), to settle for less, and you will be taken care of eventually. Work ethic has drastically decreased throughout the years. This is shown everywhere you look.

For example, many people who immigrate to this country, legally or illegally, don't make a valiant effort to learn the language. They speak their native tongue at home and around their friends and struggle to communicate with mainstream society, instead of making the effort to assimilate. Everywhere you turn, you are being asked if you want the menu for whatever it may be in Spanish or English. Sometimes I have even been told to press one for Spanish (Para Español, oprima numero uno) and press two for English. This is America; learn the language or leave! This goes for all languages, not just Spanish. If I moved to your country and worked in your economy, then I would make a valiant effort to speak your language. By adding Spanish or any other language to a menu in a restaurant or on an American phone line for an American company, you are furthering the infestation of people who feel they don't need to learn the language in this country. Don't you dare call yourself an American if you can't assimilate and stand for the American way. For you business owners who implement these multilingual menus, your profits are more important than your patriotism—shame on you.

In the early 1900s, people came here in droves and had an incredible drive to make their own way. It was completely honorable for someone to be a steelworker or dockhand then, but now it's considered manual labor for uneducated people who can't do anything else. Some of the best, smartest, and most patriotic Americans out there still work these hard jobs. The real problem is, now people "work hard" in an office, but they're sitting at a desk all day; how hard can it be? I understand everyone experiences stress on the job, and most people are committed to providing for their families. But as hard as it feels, always remember you have it easy compared to the men and women fighting for this country every day. I've come to the realization that people need to stop saying things like, "My job is killing me," when I have one that kills many for your right to say something that stupid. Having been in my profession for over eight years now, I know what hard work is. I know what it is like to have it really tough, and believe it or not, I have put in quite a few twenty-hour days behind a desk.

My best friend, Bunker, drove a desk for a few years in New York's competitive business world. While I have a great deal of respect for him and the long hours and intensive work he put in, he would tell you himself that he had it easy. He decided to quit and take a job with an American company that moved him to Africa for almost a year to help coffee farmers and other local workers establish more efficient international businesses. Talk about selfless and an asset to society. He now owns a health food company called Lesser Evil that provides a healthy alternative to most junk food. He saw a need for healthy snack alternatives, and he capitalized on it; that's what the American way is all about.

The problem is that there are so many people making their millions today by sitting behind a desk, but when they come home and there is firewood to be split for Christmas morning, they go to the store and buy it—point being that working in an office is one thing, but you still need to be able to man up and do some physical labor and have basic skills of mankind. Let us not forget that men, though society has tried to dictate otherwise, are by nature still the protectors. The business world is softening up today's society, and a 125-pound lawyer feels that he can talk down to a 250-pound dockhand. And the ability for people to do work around the house or change their own oil is disappearing. Remember your roots always.

THE CONSTITUTION

With crooked lawyers and bought-off senators these days, freedom is getting to be more of a conditional thing than ever before. Laws, the Constitution, and its amendments are getting twisted around to accommodate whatever the current administration's ideas and desires are. Look at how the Democrats are disassembling and restricting the Second Amendment while they try to expand the others. You can't pick and choose what to support; officials are elected and sworn into office to *uphold* the Constitution. What part of "uphold" do you not understand? This includes you military commanders, who think that you can just do whatever you want, regardless of people's rights (more on that later). People who were far more invested in this country than anyone alive today thought up those standards and put them on paper for this country to abide and live by, because they saw what can happen when a country and its government does not have those laws—deal with it. You don't like it? Leave. I know I've preached about acting on your passion to change something, but this is like arguing with a stop sign. It's there, and it's gotten us this far. By trying to rewrite the Constitution, you are breaking down the foundations that made America the greatest nation in the world, and just in case there was a need to change it, our forefathers left a way to amend or even add to our founding document. It's sickening how both sides of the aisle twist the words of the Constitution to mean what they want at the moment.

> By trying to rewrite the Constitution, you are breaking down the foundations that made America the greatest nation in the world.

Let's discuss a few articles and amendments that have been misread and twisted by some of our national leaders.

Article 2, section 2 of the Constitution: "The President shall be Commander in Chief of the Army and Navy of the United States, and of the Militia of the several States. . . ."[3]

Now how in the world is someone supposed to command the most powerful and advanced military in the world without ever having any experience serving in it? It should be mandated that if you want to serve as a US senator, congressman, or president, you should serve in the military first. It's your right not to serve, but those who haven't probably should not speak up too much about how war and international conflicts are handled, due to their inexperience in such matters. I know you don't have to know how to flip a burger to own a McDonald's, but you should have flipped a burger to run a McDonald's. In the military or any other organization, you do your time in the trenches, so to speak, before you run the show.

Article 2, section 4: "The President, Vice President and all civil Officers of the United States, shall be removed from Office on Impeachment for, and Conviction of, Treason, Bribery, or other high Crimes and Misdemeanors."[4]

Well, seeing how our current president was voted *into* office with a published statement written by his own hand about how he did cocaine, the likelihood of his being convicted of it now is highly unlikely. It blows my mind that people not only ignored that fact, but they raised him up as "a man of the people" for it, while Sarah Palin was crucified as a barbarian because she hunts wild game—a perfectly legal and civil act, mind you. And how about all the senators President Obama bribed with your tax dollars to vote for his health care agenda? Or going to war with Libya without congressional approval? Take your pick.

Article 3, section 3: "Treason against the United States shall consist only in levying War against them, or in adhering to their Enemies, giving them Aid and Comfort. No Person shall be convicted of Treason unless on the Testimony of two Witnesses to the same overt Act, or on Confession in open Court."[5]

Before writing this, I have to take a deep breath. Our current administration and other foreign governments want to shut down Guantanamo Bay holding facility and stop "torturing" our prisoners of war for information, because they think it is wrong. Only recently did President Obama change his mind by signing the *National Defense Authorization Act*. What was the problem? Proposals were thrown out to bring them into United States prisons, because no one else wants them. Not even the countries that are griping about keeping them at Guantanamo are willing to take custody of them. Prisoners today are given three meals a day, a temperate place to live, better medical attention than most of our citizens, and a bed in which to sleep. Is that not giving them aid and comfort? Does anyone in power see this? Our leniency is mocked every day and broadcast across the entire world, yet nothing is done to those who mock it. The underwear bomber is a perfect example. That guy tried to blow up a plane full of Americans, admitted doing it in the name of his religion, and Attorney General Eric Holder mandated that he be read Miranda rights. The bomber's behavior was an act of war or treason—pick one. At that point, he should have been considered an enemy combatant, tried by the military, and treated as such, no debate.

Article 5: "The Congress, whenever two thirds of both Houses shall deem it necessary, shall propose Amendments to this Constitution, or, on the Application of the Legislatures of two thirds of the several States, shall call a Convention for proposing Amendments, which, in either Case, shall be valid to all Intents and Purposes, as Part of this Constitution, when ratified by the Legislatures of three-fourths of the several States, or by Conventions in three-fourths thereof, as the one or the other Mode of Ratification may be proposed by the Congress; Provided that no Amendment which may be made prior to the Year One thousand eight hundred and eight shall in any Manner affect the first and fourth Clauses in the Ninth Section of the first Article; and that no State, without its Consent, shall be deprived of its equal Suffrage in the Senate."[6]

This means that, if you don't like a current amendment or article, there is a proper way to modify or take that away. Nowhere does it say that, if you don't like it, you can just make stupid conditions, stipulations, and taxes, like the ones being proposed to the Second Amendment to impose personal views on the public. To put things in terms politicians can understand, doing so will make law-abiding people not vote for you again.

AMENDMENTS

Let's move on to some amendments. The first ten amendments of the United States Constitution are more commonly referred to as the Bill of Rights, because they set forth specific rights of every American that our founders believed were granted by God and not given by man. They believed that a right given by man could be taken by man, but one given by God could only be taken by God. Rights are things that a person is entitled to and no one can take away (for you confused politicians who think that your skewed interpretation and daily gut feeling is morally higher than the Constitution).

The First Amendment: "Congress shall make no law respecting an establishment of religion, or prohibiting the free exercise thereof; or abridging the freedom of speech, or of the press; or the right of the people peaceably to assemble, and to petition the Government for a redress of grievances."[7]

Being a fairly opinionated person, I tend to voice my view, which in the military is not always good for my career. On that, I consider this book to be a peaceful grievance of how the government has run this country recently. Am I not entitled to that? Every measure I took to

> Our founders believed that a right given by man could be taken by man, but one given by God could only be taken by God.

publish this book was met with stalling and threats of legal repercussion by my superiors. Could that be considered not "upholding the constitution"?

Also, why is it that people like former National Public Radio (NPR) reporter Juan Williams are being fired for exercising their right to free speech in a logical manner by an organization that receives federal funding, while it is perfectly fine for someone else to stomp on our flag? I consider that flag an icon of the United States, so is destroying it not outside the realm of peaceful assembly?

And consider the Christmas war that was so greatly addressed by personal favorite Bill O'Reilly. Many schools and stores and even parades have been forced to take Christmas pageants, decorations, and verbiage out of the curriculum. It offends people? Well, it offends me that you are offended. What about how I feel? Is that not prohibiting the freedom to exercise religion?

The Second Amendment. (Oh, I do love this one. Nancy Pelosi and other gun law dreamers, I am about to blow your mind.) "A well regulated Militia being necessary to the security of a Free State, the right of the people to keep and bear Arms shall not be infringed."[8]

Yeehaw! I'm allowed to own all the guns I want! A well-regulated militia is a call to arms of nonmilitary personnel to help support the state. And as a current military person, who will one day be a civilian again, I just might be called to arms, a call that I would answer faster than Al Sharpton can declare something racist.

Nancy Pelosi did warn the public to be mindful of returning soldiers and their right-wing extremist style. Let's cover that quickly: men and women had just come back to their homeland after putting their lives on the line to defend its citizens, policies, and beliefs, and she could stand up and "warn" the public about returning soldiers. Give me a break! Even if the heroes returning from war did rise up with our guns, it would be *for* the country and not *against* it; take that as you will. This is probably why the American people threw Pelosi out of power during the 2010 midterm election; if she's dumb enough to say something like that, who knows what else she would do to the country—maybe spend over two million dollars of your money having the air force fly her around and serve her chocolate-covered strawberries (yeah, that happened). If you don't believe in fighting, it's because you have never had to fight for anything. But since I have, don't lecture me and those like me on whether we need to be ready to fight as a last resort.

"The right . . . shall not be infringed." I don't know how you can misread or twist that. Fortunately, our forefathers were smarter than all you antigun fairies, so they made it pretty cut and dried. This in no way means taxing ammunition heavily to get people to stop shooting. It takes one bullet to kill someone. Just ask Jared Loughner, the Arizona shooter; I'm sure he would have bought that ammo, no matter what it cost. If I wanted to kill someone, I would pay the obscene tax on that bullet to do it. The only people you are hurting by this ridiculousness are lawful, safe gun owners, who shoot as recreation or for food.

What is even more disturbing and illegal is President Obama's new attempt to eviscerate more of the Second Amendment by launching a new gun-control offensive that will allow the executive branch to issue orders in regard to firearms, bypassing the congressional approval, falling in suit with his dictator-style rule. What's next? Are you going to ban kitchen knives because violent crimes are being committed with those too? I ran across a great article that really breaks down the true values of carrying a gun. Everything the author says reflects what I and most other law-abiding gun owners think, just expressed in a more articulate manner.

The Gun Is Civilization
by Marko Kloos

Human beings only have two ways to deal with one another: reason and force. If you want me to do something for you, you have a choice of either convincing me via argument, or forcing me to do your bidding under threat of force. Every human interaction falls into one of those two categories, without exception. Reason or force, that's it.

In a truly moral and civilized society, people exclusively interact through persuasion. Force has no place as a valid method of social interaction, and the only thing that removes force from the menu is the personal firearm, as paradoxical as it may sound to some.

When I carry a gun, you cannot deal with me by force. You have to use reason and try to persuade me, because I have a way to negate your threat or employment of force. The gun is the only personal weapon that puts a 100-pound woman on equal footing with a 220-pound mugger, a 75-year-old retiree on equal footing with a 19-year-old gangbanger, and a single guy on equal footing with a carload of drunk guys with baseball bats. The gun removes the disparity in physical strength, size, or numbers between a potential attacker and a defender.

There are plenty of people who consider the gun as the source of bad force equations. These are the people who think that we'd be more civilized if all guns were removed from society, because a firearm makes it easier for a mugger to do his job. That, of course, is only true if the mugger's potential victims are mostly disarmed, either by choice or by legislative fiat—it has no validity when most of a mugger's potential marks are armed.

People who argue for the banning of arms ask for automatic rule by the young, the strong, and the many, and that's the exact opposite of a civilized society. A mugger, even an armed one, can only make a successful living in a society where the state has granted him a force monopoly.

Then there's the argument that the gun makes confrontations lethal that otherwise would only result in injury. This argument is fallacious in several ways. Without guns involved, confrontations are won by the physically superior party inflicting overwhelming injury on the loser.

People who think that fists, bats, sticks, or stones don't constitute lethal force watch too much TV, where people take beatings and come out of it with a bloody lip at worst. The fact that the gun makes lethal force easier works solely in favor of the weaker defender, not the stronger attacker. If both are armed, the field is level.

The gun is the only weapon that's as lethal in the hands of an octogenarian as it is in the hands of a weight lifter. It simply wouldn't work as well as a force equalizer if it weren't both lethal and easily employable.

When I carry a gun, I don't do so because I am looking for a fight, but because I'm looking to be left alone. The gun at my side means that I cannot be forced, only persuaded. I don't carry it because I'm afraid, but because it enables me to be unafraid. It doesn't limit the actions of those who would interact with me through reason, only the actions of those who would do so by force. It removes force from the equation . . . and that's why carrying a gun is a civilized act.

So the greatest civilization is one where all citizens are equally armed and can only be persuaded, never forced.[9]

Many people oppose that logic; that is, until they need to defend their own or their family's lives, as in the case of Senator R. C. Soles just outside of Tabor City, North Carolina. While at home with his family, two intruders attempted to enter the senator's home, and Mr. Soles responded by shooting and wounding one of the criminals. While that is an adequate and more than reasonable response to such a situation, it was a textbook hypocritical action. That particular senator, a long-term seat-holder, had supported many movements against gun ownership for the public. This is a classic example of the progressive government's thinking that they know better than the American people. Or maybe he believes his family and his personal safety are more important than yours or mine.[10]

By the people, for the people, huh? I guess we are just a bunch of stupid citizens who don't know any better. Well, "Do as I say, not as I do" seems to be the theme of most of the left side of the aisle.

Look at Washington DC, it has one of the highest violent crime rates in the country, yet for so long, you couldn't own (and still can't carry) a handgun. Abundant gun laws endanger the law-abiding citizens more than they help them. Chicago and Los Angeles also have some of the highest violent crime rates, and they make legal gun ownership and carry rights nearly impossible. Other states that have fewer firearms restrictions generally have lower violent crime rates. Look at Vermont, for example. If someone knows that you may be carrying a gun, then the likelihood of his attacking you is substantially lower. I carry a gun almost everywhere I go. Do I expect or look forward to using it? Of course not, but it's better to have it and not need it than to need it and not have it.

> If you don't like guns, then don't buy them, and when the time comes for you to need one, come see me; I have plenty.

Bottom line: if you don't like guns, then don't buy them, and when the time comes for you to need one, come see me; I have plenty. While we are on the topic of gun rights being taken away, let's look at the Fourth Amendment.

Amendment 4: "The right of the people to be secure in their persons, houses, papers, and effects, against unreasonable searches and seizures, shall not be violated, and no Warrants shall issue, but upon probable cause, supported by Oath or affirmation, and particularly describing the place to be searched, and the persons or things to be seized."[11]

This means that, because the Second Amendment allows me to own guns, the Fourth Amendment means you can't take them away for no reason. Chalk another one up for the good guys.

These are just a few examples of different interpretations of our highest legal document. There are many other things that may not be in the Constitution because some issues today are so crazy that our forefathers thought common sense would always prevail. I am sorry to say, Mr. Franklin, you gave modern politicians too much credit. For example, gay marriage—love is love, give me a break. My views of homosexuality are very straightforward: I don't like it, and I think it is a major flaw of society. My views are based on a few life experiences. First, when I was a young boy, I was molested by my gymnastics coach, someone both my parents and I trusted. Second, my uncle died of AIDS because he was gay and blamed it on the world. Third, the Bible forbids it, as demonstrated in these verses from the King James Version:

> For this cause God gave them up unto vile affections: for even their women did change the natural use into that which is against nature: And likewise also the men, leaving the natural use of the woman, burned in their lust one toward another; men with men working that which is unseemly, and receiving in themselves that recompense of their error which was meet. (Romans 1:26–27)

> Thou shalt not lie with mankind, as with womankind: it is abomination. (Leviticus 18:22)

Once again, religious or not, we live in a country founded on those morals. Bending the laws, rights, and traditions of American marriages is the wrong track for this country. Marriage is a consummation of our souls and bodies; how do two women or men consummate a marriage? Answer: they don't. While gay marriages may be legal in some states, they are in no way true marriages.

On top of that, as if it weren't lenient enough, these homosexuals want to adopt kids. Yeah, right. Do you think for one minute that anyone in his or her right mind wants to give you a child? There is a reason two same-sex partners can't reproduce or have children: they are not supposed to. I know the liberals may come back at that statement with, "Well, what about when a woman can't get pregnant naturally, and she and her husband adopt a child?" That's completely different; the woman's inability to procreate is due to a medical problem, not the basic laws of nature. It's perfectly okay when it is a mother and a father. Not two fathers or two mothers. That's just the way it is.

Homosexuality has been around since biblical times, but it has never been more widely accepted, celebrated, and embraced as it is today. This widespread acceptance is wrong and must be addressed. Homosexuality is unnatural, and why? Because same-sex couples cannot procreate. They are not made to do it, so if everyone were gay, the human race would cease to exist. Again, that's just the way it is, and to accept any other way is unacceptable.

After all these years, people at the top and bottom, Republican and Democrat, have forgotten that the government is a representation of the people, for the people. There are too many personal agendas buzzing about Capitol Hill, regardless of political party. People need to sit down and read the Constitution. While this country will evolve and change, our morals and history should not.

THREE

*Selfish, Ignorant People and
Their Effect on America*

Many people in this country, of all political views, don't know how good they have it. It seems today that people take for granted the reliable parts of this economically gifted and fruitful nation. Things like public safety, running water, electricity, welfare, and a volunteer military that guards our American way, to name a few. People soak these things up and pay no attention to the fact that, while readily available and considered normal in our country, they are still luxuries.

While many Americans stateside are very supportive of the troops, many are not supportive of the cause for which the troops fight. Saying you support the troops but not the war is like saying you support the cure for cancer but not funding further research. Saying you support neither means you have no right to be in the country to begin with, and you are exercising the right of free speech to desecrate the very government and soldiers that allow you to have it. Not every war has a positive outcome, and you can pick apart history all you want about controversial conflicts America has engaged in, but the facts are that our leaders, who were elected by the will of the majority of Americans, took the current information presented to them and made a decision.

America, for many, is the land of opportunity. People flock from all around the world to be a part of the American culture and its freedom. It seems, aside from the extremists of the radical Muslim culture, most of the world's governments and people strive to be like America. The majority of the people who complain about this country are the ones who live here, soaking up the benefits. And I say, if you don't like it, leave.

Burning Bush

After returning home from my first deployment in October 2007, everywhere I turned people were griping about the country and the George W. Bush administration and, basically, burning him in effigy. Maybe I was just overly sensitive about antiestablishment people from my seven months at war, but I thought that was a disgrace. People who had never given anything back to this country and only did what benefits them were complaining that they had hardships because of the Bush administration. They were completely passing blame for their own faults and ignorance onto "the administration," though many of these people's hardships where brought on by themselves, just like the people (not victims) of Hurricane Katrina (more on that later).

Standing in line in a Panera Bread restaurant one day, I heard two people behind me talking about Bush, who could be seen being interviewed about Iraq on a TV mounted above the counter.

One of them said to the other, "Bush is so stupid. All we're doing over there is killing innocent people."

The other responded, "Yeah, I know, right? They are people just like us, trying to live a normal life. I feel sorry to be associated with American policy."

Mind you, I believe that these two individuals, judging from their physical appearance and their ages, would never fight for anything they believed in, as was proven in my following confrontation. Having lost three friends in close proximity during my previous deployment, I was irate and couldn't hold back.

"Have you ever been to Iraq?" I snapped at them.

"No, why?"

"Do you even know anyone who has?" I asked through clenched teeth.

"Uh, no," they snickered. "We're actually in college just so we don't have to join the military."

"Listen, you ungrateful dirtbags, I have been there and lost friends there, all three with college degrees, and if you think for one minute that we're a bunch of idiots over there, running around shooting innocent civilians, you're wrong. You are not true Americans. You're just some young punks with American citizenship who think you know everything because you watch CNN or did a three-page paper on the war in Iraq and Afghanistan."

As I turned away, I remembered one more thing. "And that nice, warm, safe feeling you have right now here in America has been provided for you by Bush, his administration, and the military, so you should quit criticizing and be grateful."

The two boys were terrified and stood there with nothing else to say. I turned around to the cashier, who had witnessed the whole conversation, and said, "I'll have a ham and Swiss on ciabatta bread with everything on it, please."

With a smirk of approval on his face, the cashier, who happened to be wearing an American flag pin on his apron, entered my order and ran my card. As I walked toward my table, I got a few looks of disgust and disapproval. Only one man in the corner with a marine-style haircut seemed to approve and shot me a thumbs-up. More people were upset with me for strongly confronting the boys than they were about those two punks smearing our nation's name. It was just another proof that this country has fallen so far from what it was founded on, and it made me a little sick to my stomach.

So many people forget that President Bush declared war on terrorism because Americans were killed in an act of war, in order to protect our homeland, and the majority of Americans *at the time* felt he had no choice. Personally, I agree with his course of action. Bush made the call to go to war

President Bush declared war on terrorism because Americans were killed in an act of war, in order to protect our homeland.

because terrorists were killing our people for no cause other than considering us "infidels." Our people's way of life was threatened. Why is it that people now want to crucify him for the decisions he made on behalf of the country that most Americans seemed to support then? If my son or daughter stood up and gave Bush's post 9/11 "We Will Not Falter" speech, I would be prouder than if I heard them recite the Gettysburg Address.

We are a very tolerant nation, even when it comes to people mocking that tolerance. In the streets of New York City, people have trampled the flag openly, and yet it is tolerated. Those people and their demonstrations are even guarded by the police, who wear that flag on their shoulder. How could people be so ignorant and hateful to a nation that allows them this much freedom? We openly accept any religion, any nationality, and any culture, yet so many of our own citizens still think we are a horrible place and there is so much wrong with the country. I have some advice for all the jerks out there who trash-talk this great country: go to North Korea and try burning their flag in the streets and see what happens. Then tell me you have a problem with America and its freedoms.

PAYING ATTENTION TO THE HOME FRONT

Another time, I was home on leave during some down time in training when my parents asked me if I would come to a cocktail party at a friend's house. The man whose house it was had previously run for political office as a Democrat and lost, so I was anxious to see what opposing opinions I would face throughout the evening. Not having any black-tie attire at hand, I decided to wear my uniform.

Arriving at the house, I soon realized, based on the amount of Bentley Rolls Royces and limos out front, that the annual income of the people attending this party was higher than most lottery jackpots. From the moment I walked in, people flocked to me to say, "Thank you for your service" and "We're so grateful to have men like you." Though most of the compliments seemed genuine, some were purely public relations statements for these highly publicized Wall Street and successful business executives. I saw right through them and their trophy wives, who could barely hold their heads up from the weight of the diamonds that shimmered on them.

Being the talkative guy that I am, I was quickly involved in a conversation with an older man, who was involved in international shipping. He seemed to genuinely support the troops, as his father had served in World War II, but like most on the left side of the aisle, he strongly opposed the war in Iraq. As we carried on a very informative (for me at least) conversation about foreign policy, some other folks made their way over to our circle.

One man said, "Hey, maybe we should stop fighting this oil war so we can start fixing our own country." Intrigued, I asked him to elaborate.

"Well, you know, we are just so inefficient here at home, depending on fossil fuels. We should spend the money from this war on alternative energy and many other things. I wish we would pay a little more attention to the home front."

As much as I would have loved to disagree with him out of spite, even though I do love my V8, 400-horsepower, gas-guzzling truck, I said, "This country does have some things that need fixing," knowing full well my idea of change and his were not even in the same library, let alone on the same page.

One of the wives, who had never worked a day in her life, chimed in, "Yeah, the government and this country are so off track that I can barely stomach paying my taxes anymore." With Bush and some of our other national leaders at the time topping my list of personal heroes, I had to make a bold retaliation to that comment.

"You think it's that bad, huh? You do know that Bush was the one who implemented tax cuts for rich folks like you? But I know why you don't like it—is it because, at any time you fall and hurt yourself, an ambulance will be there to care for you? Or is it because, if someone breaks into your house, the police will be there to protect you? Because any day of the week you can go to a grocery store and get fresh, healthy, clean food, or maybe it's that your kids can go to a state-funded school, that you don't have to shell out a dime for, and get a decent education. And even if you don't have time in your busy shopping and yoga schedule to get them there, the government-funded buses will take them there."

People around me were surprised, but some nodded in approval. The woman's comment was a classic example of ignorance.

I cite these specific instances because they sit at the top of a long list of examples that support my point of people's ignorance and selfishness; even though they have the world, they still think things are wrong. The problem is that this country has taken such good care of its people, regardless of the current administration, for so long that people have come to expect more and more and to feel they are entitled to much more than they actually are, such as those who now feel that heath care is a right. Then, when one thing is wrong, people whine. There are so many places out there that don't have nearly the rights, resources, or organization to uphold a stable way of life that America does.

HURRICANE KATRINA

Let's bring a large-scale example to the table: Hurricane Katrina. Contrary to local belief, the hurricane and its damages were not Bush's fault. This was one of the most expensive domestic natural disasters in the history of this country. We pumped millions upon millions of dollars into Gulf Coast states, especially Louisiana, through the Red Cross, the Federal Emergency Management Agency (FEMA), and military support. And what did we get out of it? When we came to rescue people via helicopter, the aircraft was shot at in one case. That was a monumental act of stupidity in America, aside from people moving to a city that is below sea level to begin with. But help was there to help you who were too stupid to heed the warning of the National Weather Service and evacuate when you were advised to leave.

Imagine watching people loot the city on the news after being told to evacuate. Then those same people were stranded on their rooftops a few days later, and when a government-funded helicopter came to pick them up, someone shot at the aircraft, which naturally flew away, leaving those people on the rooftops subjected to the elements. Can you imagine that happening? Well, it did, and then somehow it reflected on the government for not doing enough to help those people. The media crucified Bush and his administration. God forbid that anyone do the sensible thing without caring what the media says. So, for the greater good, I guess you could say, we continued to try to help those idiots. At what point do you say, (1) "You should have evacuated a coastal city *below* sea level prior to a category-five hurricane when directed," and (2) "Sorry, a few of you ruined it for all of you. Have a nice day"?

Even for the subsequent year after the disaster, many people, who had been given an open-ended ticket, were still living in hotels while Uncle Sam (your tax dollars and mine) fronted the bill. Crazy? I think it is. I just want to shake those people, look them in the eye, and legitimately ask them if they realize they are a drain on the economy and bring nothing to the table. Though quite a few people took only the help that they needed and moved on and continued to make their own way again, many did not. For those of you who did that, thank you for being responsible; the next step you can take to contributing to society further is telling those human parasites who did otherwise to get their acts together.

BATTLE ON THE HOME FRONT

HEALTH AND FITNESS

A more common type of laziness I see often, that many people don't even give a second thought to, is people not taking care of their health. Something I am so passionate about, due in part to my current occupation, is fitness. Every day I see more overweight people simply because they are lazy and careless. I always hear about how it's okay to be fat as long as you are comfortable with yourself, true beauty is on the inside, and garbage like that. A fat, ugly person probably thought up those slogans and others like them. Guess what. Being fat is not okay; it's selfish. I will explain, using a real-world experience.

I was getting on a plane to come back from doing some training with the military when I saw an enormous woman drinking a sixty-four-ounce soda in the airport, waiting to get on the same plane. I thought, *I really hope I don't have to sit next to her.* Well, fate frowned on me that day, and shortly after I had sat down, so did she. I had the window, and she had the aisle.

Being compressed in the normal-sized coach seat, she turned to me and said, "Can you put up the arm rest?"

I replied, "No. If you're too fat to fit in one seat, you should have bought two," thinking that, since I'm just shy of six feet tall and 240 pounds, with a very large build, and I have no problem fitting into a seat, then there is no reason why anyone else, especially a woman six inches shorter than me, should be so big she needs to put up the arm rest so she can ooze over into my space.

With a look of disgust at being faced with reality, she rang the call button. As the attendant came around, the now perspiring woman asked for a seatbelt extension. I couldn't believe my ears.

"Lady, have you tried dieting?" I asked calmly, remembering the extra-large soda she inhaled prior to boarding.

"I have a thyroid problem," she snapped at me.

"No, you have an eating problem. I saw you slam a massive soda while you were waiting to board the plane!"

42

Really? This raises another issue that we face as a nation: excuses. Though it is entirely understandable to have a medical problem that would make you gain weight faster than others, it is still rarely an excuse for being fat, and it all comes down to simple math. Fact: if you don't eat fat-based food, you won't gain weight. If you maintain a calorie-deficient diet (meaning you consume fewer calories than you burn), you will lose weight.

Even beyond weight issues, too many people blame their problems on issues that society has deemed acceptable. Someone sometime decided that it was okay to be fat, and they must have been famous enough to appeal to a lot of people, and now, combined with the fact that there is a fast-food restaurant on every street corner, more than half the country is obese. This costs the taxpayers untold amounts of money every year in medical expenses. For that reason alone, people should be taking personal responsibility to slim down. To make matters worse, modern society has deemed it morally wrong to say anything disheartening, no matter how true it is. Here's an idea for all you people who are "short for your weight" (to use a politically correct phrase): break up that hour a day you spend getting ready for work, and take thirty minutes to exercise and thirty minutes to get ready.

> America, it's time to start being more responsible about your weight.

Fat people are contagious as well. Chances are that, if you have fat friends, you will become like them, and the reverse goes for having fit friends, and here is why. If you have a fat friend, most of the activities you do together will be sedentary and require little to no physical stimulation, hence the reason they are fat. Also, you tend to adjust to their diet plans. Consequently, you will most likely gain weight while adopting their habits. The same philosophy goes for fat parents and their children. If the parents eat junk food all day and lie around the house, then the children will be brought up with the same mentality. America, it's time to start being more responsible about your weight.

OVERPOPULATION

Another issue that hinders America and the rest of the world is people having too many children. This ranges from low-income families trying to get a larger welfare check to rich bureaucrats. Two hundred years ago, it might have made sense to have as many kids as possible, due to the low survival rate of people who contracted sicknesses, such as the common cold, but today there is no need for that. Two, three, or even four kids are acceptable, but any more than that is contributing to the overpopulation of this planet.

As always, there are exceptions, such as when a couple has children born through a previous marriage, which makes another kid or two a responsible decision as long as they can be supported. As for the low-income families who have tons of kids, my question is why? If you can't adequately support a child or children, don't have them. If that means not having sex, then so be it. In the end, you are going to just end up costing the taxpayers money because you were too stupid and selfish to think ahead. Even the rich, who have no problem supporting five or more kids, are contributing to the burden of this planet. I am in no way suggesting a law like China's, but I'm simply asking that people take more personal responsibility. Earth and America can only sustain so much. So as much as you want to have a bunch of kids, for their sakes, don't, because they are the ones who are going to have to deal with the overpopulation issues when they grow up. Many people think, *well, it's just one kid*. But guess what: there are millions of couples out there, and if every one of them had six kids instead of three or four, then those numbers will add up. For this reason, we all need to do our part.

SUPPORTING CHILDREN

This goes along with my next topic, children out of wedlock. Too many people today have kids and are not sticking around to raise or properly support them. Bottom line: if you have a child, it is your responsibility to raise that child, whether you meant to conceive or not. There are no exceptions to this. If you can't support a child, you find a way, because you found a way to have sex, and the child is the result. You can't punish a child for your mistake or irresponsibility. That's the way it is. Child support violations need to be treated much more harshly than they are today.

HOLLYWOOD "STARS"

Probably the worst of all are actors and other Hollywood icons. I will touch more on this later, but these people are getting progressively dumber for the most part, and the media just gives them more airtime for it. Look at Paris Hilton, who is essentially famous because her dad is rich, and her everyday life of being pampered and drunk seemed amusing enough to do what they call a "reality" show, covering the events and antics of her life. Here's the kicker: these are the types of people who get the most publicity. No wonder our younger generations are acting as they are. It's because of these "stars." They are raised up as icons of society, and when asked their political views, which they always are, their answers are taken as gospel by the youth of the nation. Problem? I think so.

DO SOMETHING!

Give an American a rope, and he'll want to be a cowboy, right? Well, not exactly. Most Americans want to say they are cowboys until they have to lasso the cows. A growing problem today is that everyone talks the talk, but few walk the walk. There are tons of people who are tough guys on a sunny

Saturday afternoon when the going is good, but if it starts to rain, it washes away those muscles. Put your money where your mouth is. Don't just read this book and agree with me—act on it. Say something the next time you see someone being worthless; don't stand idly by as a person with nine kids and a brand-new iPhone is using food stamps to buy groceries. Speak out! If you claim to be a patriot, sack up, because America needs you now more than ever. There are many ways to contribute to the improvement of society. Just keep that in mind when you make decisions in your best interest.

FOUR

Racism, Sexism, Prejudice, and Stereotypes

During the founding years of this country, not all people were treated "right." There was the cruelty toward and slaughter of Native Americans and slavery, to name two major ones. Since then, we have come a long way. The Indians were given some compensation, and Lincoln freed the slaves at the cost of six hundred thousand American lives.

Since the development of this country, we have moved closer and closer to equality. Somewhere between then and now, though, we have started moving in reverse, and the current president—who was supposed to *unite* this country—has drawn lines and divided us more than ever before. Certain races and cultures are actually getting ahead by claiming that, if they don't get a leg up, then it's racism or prejudice. Guess what—no one alive today has ever legally suppressed or enslaved anyone else who is alive today. Get over it, and make your own way.

It pains me to say this, but look at President Obama, who won the presidential election while our country was at war with radical Islam. That shows that anyone can do anything they set their minds to as long as they play their cards right. You won't hear this from me again, so soak it up, Obama zombies: well done, Mr. President—you have obtained something remarkable. I say that with no sarcasm and the utmost seriousness.

More proof of this being an equal world is Oprah Winfrey. She is one of the richest people in the world, contributes millions to charity and other helpful causes, and she has gotten no leg up for being black. She did support President Obama, but no one is perfect.

EQUALITY?

Having given my praises where due, I will jump back on my horse. Nowadays, there are affirmative action, black colleges, Hispanic organizations, the NAACP, and black history month. There are no white colleges, no white history month, and more often than you would think, when a white male scores higher on some entrance exam, he does *not* get the job. Why? Because the organization doesn't have enough Hispanics or blacks to meet its "desired quota." What is a desired quota? I thought we were all equal. I know firsthand, because a good friend of mine returned from a tour in Iraq as a marine, applied and took the test for a Connecticut police department, and though he scored third highest among the group applying, he was not accepted to one of the four spots available. Two nonwhite people got those third and fourth positions. Does anyone see anything wrong with this kind of garbage? Is this not racism at its core, too, denying a qualified white applicant a job based on race?

> Is this not racism at its core, too, denying a qualified white applicant a job based on race?

It's much like the Connecticut firefighters' case in early 2009 in which twenty white firefighters filed a lawsuit claiming racism. The city of New

Haven said it did not count many of the white people's exams because no minorities would have been promoted based on an equal system. This violates the equal protection clause of the United States Constitution and Title VII of the Civil Rights Act, which forbids discrimination because of race. Before the Civil Rights Movement, there was a genuine need to bring minorities into positions, because they might not have had the opportunity for the same education that more fortunate white people had. But now? There is a double standard, and it honestly makes me sick. There has been ample time for anyone in this country today to overcome any hardship or racial disadvantage they might have had in the past. It seems that, whenever something bad happens to a black person, it's a hate crime, and Rev. Al Sharpton jumps in to give his moral support and opinion. Go home, Reverend, you only make things worse. That is probably why, on one occasion, 100 percent of *The O'Reilly Factor's* viewers voted him a "pinhead."

Take the instance of a few years ago when two black boys in Belleville, Illinois, beat up a seventeen-year-old white boy while other black students cheered them on. That incident was passed off as general bullying. Or when an Ohio man, Marty Marshall, and his family, were beaten by a mob of black teenagers screaming, "This is a black world!" Why were these not immediately declared racially motivated crimes? If the roles had been reversed, the perpetrators would have been called a lynch mob or white supremacists. Things like that seem to stand out as mockeries of our so-called equality. What part of *equal opportunity* is not understood these days?

One of my close friends was black and a Navy SEAL; I served with him for four years. There is only a handful of black active duty SEALs at any given time, mostly because black people notoriously can't swim. (This is not my opinion—it is a fact that most black applicants to BUD/S do not pass the swim portion of the preliminary screening.) But you know what? He set his mind to a goal and met the same standards everyone else met. He deserves to be there as much as anyone else. On top of that, any SEAL, including me, would take a bullet for him just as fast as we would for anyone else. He is a good man with whom I am honored to have served. He did not need, nor did he accept, any leg up to get where he is today.

UNIONS

Let's talk about some of the *smoothly* running organizations today that were founded on the basis of racism, specifically unions. They went from destroying one race to now destroying a whole country and its economic growth. The history and origins of these corrupt organizations are skewed. In addition to protecting people from getting fired for being lazy, and making our wages higher than anywhere else in the world, giving us little to no competitive edge in a global market, they were founded on the basis of racism.

One of the first organized labor unions in the United States was formed in 1877. It was Dennis Kearney's California Working Man's Party, and it was founded on crushing the Chinese workers on the West Coast. In fact, their slogan was, "The Chinese must go." He made such statements as, "We intend to try to vote the Chinaman out, to frighten him out, and if this won't do, to kill him out."

Between the Civil War and World War I, unions blatantly excluded blacks. How is it okay to have organizations with roots like that still thriving today? While the general focus of unions today is protecting their workers from doing hard work and working in "unjust" conditions, it truly protects and embraces laziness. It is nearly impossible to fire someone from a unionized organization today. Don't believe me? Next time you drive by a section of road construction, count how many people are working and how many are standing around. In what way has this been beneficial to the country? Thank God for people like the New Jersey governor, Chris Christie, who is willing to put his foot down. Wisconsin also had the right idea, but unfortunately, all the Democrats were derelict of their duties while still collecting a paycheck and left the state so a vote could not be held. Even more amazing, after jumping ship for almost a month, those senators who left still have a job.

Speaking of criminal, there are many ways for people in general to be successful in society without mirroring the criminal image. For instance, many blacks today are extremely athletic, which can be traced back to the fact that slaves were bred and chosen from the strongest males and females. I certainly don't agree with slavery, but I do think that you should play the hand you are dealt, and good physical genetics are definitely dealt to many blacks. I have seen young men growing up in the ghetto with amazing athletic potential, but because of the environment or lack of positive influence, they never have a chance to exploit it. There are also kids of all nationalities growing up in these poor neighborhoods, who are smart but throw it away on drugs and gangs, because that is the only thing they know. They fall into the pattern of destruction because they think it is cool. If they want to, they can get out of that type of life. They don't have to be druggies, but they have to want to put in the extra effort to do better for themselves. Parents in those situations, it wouldn't hurt for you to step up as well.

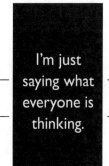

I'm just saying what everyone is thinking.

Too often these days, racism is taken too far, such as in the case of Senator Harry Reid, the Democrat Senate majority leader. He referred to the slang that is typically used by black people as "Negro dialect." As much as I would have liked to see him resign from office, I did not think that was such a big deal. I understand that the GOP found an opportunity to disgrace the left, but come on, the Dems have messed up enough stuff in their last reign of terror to make them look bad. Use some of that ammunition; don't dig for stuff. The bottom line here is, the comment he made was in a complimentary context. Besides, everyone knows about the "Negro dialect"; how else do you classify the Ebonics/

slang used by most of the black community? I'm just saying what everyone is thinking. Since I'm on a roll with stating the obvious, let's discuss stereotypes.

STEREOTYPES

While embraced by society, stereotypes are also furthered by whatever race or group is in question. Let's take the black rap image of "money, hoes, and convicts." All these things are clearly and proudly depicted in most rap videos. While there are some rappers out there who discourage this type of negativity, most embrace it. As an American role model, making music videos, swinging gold chains and grinning gold teeth, degrading women, and talking about drugs and crime as if they are cool, how do you think people are going to classify those who mirror your image? Is that what you want people to see, especially "your people," as they are frequently called? Kids try to imitate the things they see and hear, and they get into trouble as a result, and in some cases, killed. When you incorporate the sound of a gun slide-chambering a round and automatic gunfire as part of your chorus, do you seriously think that makes you sound tough or more "gangsta"?

Why is it so widely broadcast by rap that it is a matter of bragging rights to have a criminal record? Hello, you are bringing down society and the very people who embrace your ways. Guys like 50 Cent—are you serious? You got shot in the face, lived to tell about it, then went on to write a song mocking those who did it. How stupid are you? If they did it once, guess what? Mocking them will probably make them want to do it again and make sure they finish the job this time. If you really had a problem with the way you grew up in the "hood," don't entice people to live like that through your image. You wonder how stereotypes are made? Well, here you go. If you take the majority of people and/or public icons of a certain group, and they all come off as uneducated criminals, then everybody who emulates that will be associated with that stereotype.

Things like sagging your pants is in no way comfortable or functional. I tried it for a day, just to see what all the hype was about. During that day, I did some research online, and I found out that when inmates in prison get outside for their interactive recess, if you are gay and available, you openly sag your pants as a signal. Also, prior to the current elastic waistbands, inmates were not allowed to have belts (to avoid suicides). As a result, their pants were often loose to the point of falling down. In addition, most prisons have generic sizes that are on the bigger end of the sizing charts, so they are bigger and baggier. In fact, the baggy pants went right along with the prison fashion line—inmates were given overly baggy pants so that, if they escaped, they could not run without tripping. Even on the outside, persons attempting to conceal items often make this fashion statement.

> If you have oversized, saggy, baggy clothes, you look like a thug. . . . Open your eyes! You will never get ahead in the real world looking like a thug.

I'm not the only one who feels this way. Even influential black people, such as Bill Cosby, are ridiculed and called "sell outs" because they thinks issues such as dialect and sagging pants are as stupid as I do. Mr. Cosby is a tremendous asset to society and a traditionalist; yet, he is made to look as if he's forgotten where he came from because he thinks the black community is not benefitting from the rap culture.

Any way you slice it, if you have oversized, saggy, baggy clothes, you look like a thug. It's not fashionable, but here are the kids who follow the rap culture—many in lower-income classes—wearing those pants. Open your eyes! You can't expect to get ahead looking like a thug—outside of the one in ten million chance you land a rap contract.

And while on the topic of the rap culture, let's tackle a word that is forbidden by white people but widely accepted as cool talk by black kids—"nigger" or as it is more commonly said, "nigga."

This is a very sore topic for me. The word "negro" means black in Spanish. I understand where it comes from, just as I understand where the term "cracker" is derived, as in the white slave owner who would "crack" the whip. I'm not holding a press conference if someone is stupid enough to call me that, but I certainly would not be caught calling my friends that either. So why do black kids think it's cool to call each other "nigga" and other racial slurs?

If this is such a big deal for white people to use that word, why is the same word used as some form of friendly greeting among black people? That's the benefit of this rap culture—thug life, gangsta vibe—and as I said, there are black people who agree with me. In fact, most blacks, Hispanics and whites who were born before the 1970's don't find this lifestyle appealing. Why should you?

RACIAL PROFILING

Racial profiling came from this thug image. If you look like a thug, talk like a thug, and act like a thug, then guess what? You are a thug, regardless of whether you are white, black, brown, yellow, or green. Why is it such a crime these days to stop someone who is of Middle Eastern descent with a turban on in an airport for security screening, considering the most recent hijacking and terrorist attacks have been from people of that descent? I haven't seen any eighty-year-old white women trying to light their shoes on fire, so why is it such a big deal? If you're not a terrorist, then fine, thank you for your cooperation and we'll send you on your way. You should feel good that people are looking out for your security in an intelligent manner. Also, if you don't like it, either don't fly, or leave.

Look at what happened to Juan Williams from NPR. He was really fired for appearing on Fox, but NPR said they fired him for saying, "When I get on the plane, I got to tell you, if I see people who are in Muslim garb, and I think, you know, they are identifying themselves first and foremost as Muslims, I get worried. I get nervous." Juan had every right to say what he did. Why should that offend anyone? If I hear someone say to me, "When I see you carrying a gun, I get nervous," I don't care. I just tell them things are probably safer with my having one, but I don't throw a hissy fit. If I see someone walking down the street with a turban on his head, that's his right, but it is also my right to be suspicious, along with Juan. That's especially true with the current threat status in America, but people really don't care to see that. Maybe one hundred years ago this was the "melting pot," but not anymore. We have our own culture and customs here. What you do in your house is your business, but if you walk out on the street, don't complain about how people might profile you. There are plenty of ways to assimilate into our culture while still embracing yours and not standing out in a negative way.

Having done ride-alongs with the Boston Police Department, I have seen firsthand that racial profiling works. For instance, we were on patrol, and we saw a Hispanic male with gold chains, a gold watch, and a giant fur coat in a brand-new Lexus.

One of the officers said, "We would love to pull that guy over and check him out, but our hands are tied." The current chief was a big equal-opportunity guy at the time. No sooner had he said that to me than the same guy shot the middle finger to the cops and punched the accelerator, warranting pulling him over. When the officer approached the car, it smelled of weed, and the guy was completely disrespectful. Suspicious, the officers searched his car and found enough weed to charge him with intent to sell, not to mention an illegal gun.

It makes me feel at least a little better that most of these thugs, drug dealers, and criminals are not that smart. Does driving in the ghetto with thousands of dollars of jewelry in a fifty-thousand-dollar car while in possession of drugs and an illegal gun taunt the police? Racial profiling is an effective tool, and it should be encouraged.

In context, if you saw some well-dressed preppy white guy in the hood, guess what? He's probably there to buy drugs, and I hope the police would be assertive enough to take the proper action through profiling.

The Fort Hood shooting in November 2009 could probably have been avoided had the previous instructors of Major Nidal Malik Hasan done not only profiling but also rational thinking. Though he had many noted "conflicting interests" with being a United States military officer, no one said anything, because they were too afraid of being labeled as racist or not politically correct. Now people are dead because of it. Those of you who stood by in the interest of politics, the blood of those victims is partially on your hands. One of his instructors did say something after Hasan gave a presentation justifying suicide bombers, but it was silenced at a higher level in the interest of equality and diversity. That allowed Hasan to progress to the O-4 pay grade. He essentially infiltrated the US military to the point where he would have soon been eligible to take an executive officer position. Maybe the military will think twice about being so politically correct—probably not, though, since they just opened the door for gays, cause there is no way that could possibly cause conflict, right?

Dave Chappelle is one of the best-known and funniest comedians today. I personally love his show. He has made a career of making racist jokes and playing on stereotypes. Had he been white, he would have been crucified. But in the interest of bringing these overly sensitive, racism-crying people back down to the real world, I support him. We need more people like him out there to help relax the world a little bit in the eyes of race. Thank you, Dave. Come back to fight.

JUST PLAIN AMERICANS

Have you noticed that I have consistently referred to blacks as such? Here's why. We are all citizens of America, are we not? African American, Hispanic American, Asian American—what about just plain American? I don't say I'm Italian American; I say I'm American just like every other citizen in this country, regardless of race or color. By calling yourself anything but American, you are setting yourself apart from others. Barring dual citizenship, you are either African or American, not both. The same goes for every other race. Here's the thing I find most hilarious about this whole thing. Most blacks living in America, who refer to their racial status as African American, have never even been to Africa, and in many cases, neither have their parents. You don't get much more American than that. Let it go; it's okay to be just plain old American and black.

Here is something else I don't understand. When Brazil won the World Cup in 2002, everywhere I looked the following day, Hispanics (most of whom didn't even speak English) were driving around, in America, honking their horns with Brazilian flags and loud speakers screaming that Brazil is the best and, "Viva, Brazil!" Good for you for having national pride, but if you love your home country that much, why would you be living in America? To me, that's ridiculous. If America won the World Cup, I doubt those same people, most of whom are probably American citizens, would be as expressive about it. I'm not saying it should be illegal, but it sends an interesting message about the loyalties of people.

Also, Yao Ming, a Chinese National Basketball Association (NBA) player, who plays and lives in America, and was trained by Americans, played basketball for China during the Olympics. Does anyone think someone's judgment might be a little off? I would not allow him back to play for us. But loyalty can be bought these days, I guess.

Since we are well established in our national way, why do people continue to try to make this more like the country from where they came? You left your country and came here because you thought our country is better, remember? It fires me up to no end when I see some young punk, who has lived in America his whole life, with a Puerto Rican flag in the back of his car and who can barely speak English. I mean, come on, someone else has got to see a problem with this. And maybe the parents of this kid are from Puerto Rico originally, but Puerto Rico has been supported by the United States for decades now; at least instill that in your kids, along with the English language. As I have said before, if you are so proud of your old country, then go back.

> You left your country and came here because you thought our country is better, remember?

While people technically have the right to be obnoxious and insensitive to the American way, that doesn't mean they *should* be. Another example of this was the one-hundred-million-dollar proposed Ground Zero mosque. While it is, in fact, their right to build there, in the interest of tolerance and sensitivity, they should have considered building it elsewhere. Muslims frequently complain about being hated or discriminated against and want America to be sympathetic of their ways and feelings. *Hello . . .* what about the feelings of the families of over three thousand people who were killed in the name of Allah? Muslims of America, it's things like this that will make it impossible for you to ever blend in and truly be accepted.

It may be a small minority of Muslims who want that mosque, but until there is a united, public outcry from American Muslims against it, you will inevitably be painted with the same brush. Along the same lines was Bill O'Reilly's comment on *The View.* When he was being grilled about his opposition to the Ground Zero mosque, he said, "Because Muslims killed us on 9/11." What is so wrong with that? While they were radical Muslims, they were still Muslims. Whoopi Goldberg and Joy Behar walked off *their own show* in protest to Bill's comment—just another example of how irrational these liberals are. If that's not a victory for Bill, I don't know what is. Another issue surrounding this is where the money was coming from. Again, if you want acceptance, why won't you answer the questions of how you were funding the mosque?

Taxes

Society today has taken a turn for the worse in the racial sensitivity department. People have taken things too far, and now it almost seems that it is a disadvantage to be an intelligent white person these days. Take Joe the plumber, who was so well televised during the 2008 presidential election. He was a normal guy who owned a business and who was worried about how tax hikes would affect him. If he had a good year, he would fall into a higher tax bracket. Is that not prejudice against wealthy people? Why should someone be punished or treated differently and taxed at a higher percentage than someone who makes less money? Shouldn't everyone be taxed the same percentage, regardless of their income? Anything else is essentially a punishment for being rich.

Before his campaign ended, Herman Cain was gaining momentum, as seen by the Florida Straw poll in September 2011, where he won with a crushing majority. His 9-9-9 plan of the tax breakdown drew the attention of a vast majority of sensible people. We have to understand that we can't keep taking money off the top. Someone has made all that money because they worked hard to earn it. Punishing them with higher taxes discourages the very basis of the American way, not to mention that it touches on taxation without representation.

The idea of everyone having equal opportunity is a principle the last sixty years have proven successful. Though we are all created equal, not everyone is equally as smart, strong, or capable, but the point is that everyone has equal *opportunity*, and no one can be denied anything based on race, religion, or beliefs. The false misconceptions about this principle, which has been twisted, is the line where equal opportunity meets equal achievement; they are two very different things. The funny thing is that the same people who scream for affirmative action claim that everyone is equal. If everyone is truly equal, then they should be accepted to schools and jobs based on their relative merits, not to meet a quota, as I discussed earlier in connection with the Connecticut firefighters' lawsuit. Programs and thinking like this are perpetuating the cycle of racism. This ideology breeds separation, not unity. Different people will choose to achieve more or less through different work ethics. Your lifestyle is a personal choice and a measure of how much effort you want to invest.

Women in Power

The last thing I will discuss in this chapter is women in power. Many men have a problem working for a woman. Guys, get over it. If she has earned the position, good for her. A hundred years ago, this was unheard of, but through striving for equality, I think the woman's position in society has changed for the better. What I do not agree with is women thinking they can physically do everything a man can do. I understand that there are women who are physically bigger, faster, and stronger than some men. Guess what? Those weaker men should not apply for the physically demanding jobs either.

For example, in the interest of their safety, most female police officers should not work alone, generally speaking. I happen to think that men shouldn't either, but if someone has to work alone, it should be the most physically robust person in the department, which is likely a man. When I had six kids break into my house one night from a party down the street of nearly two hundred sixteen- to twenty-two-year-old kids, I naturally dealt with the six in my house violently, while my wife called the cops. Now, you would think the response to a call from a woman saying, "Six kids broke into my house, and my husband is downstairs with his gun dealing with it" would warrant more than one barely five-foot-tall female police officer, right? Well, not that night.

This is the problem: there has been such a surge for equality that people get themselves into bad spots. And that is a fault of many people more interested in winning an image war than actually thinking about how things will play out in real life. There are plenty of female icons today that did great things. But certain things women have strived for these days are not appropriate roles for women. Take submarines for example. Until recently, women were not allowed to serve in the navy's submarine community. That was not because the navy was trying to hold women back; it was because submarines are so cramped that it doesn't allow for the respectable berthing and separation of females from the rest of the male crew. My point is that, as men, we have a role to fill, and so do women. While that role could be CEO or mom, it is vital that everyone does his or her part correctly and appropriately.

I know some of the things I have said in this chapter may make people angry, but I have always been a firm believer in getting your point out there in the straightest way possible and not taking too much time to bother about whether or not you offend people. If it does offend you, get over it, or stop reading this book. This is the cold truth about racial and gender conflict these days. Someone needed to come out and say what most people have been thinking without beating around the bush.

FIVE

Past Idols and Modern Media Heroes

I have touched on a few of my next topics in the past chapters, but I would like to elaborate a little more in a different context. The standard of society can be fairly accurately judged by those who are held up as idols, such as movie stars and fashion icons, to name two.

Movie Stars

Let's address movie stars first. Thirty years ago, who were our action stars? There was Arnold Schwarzenegger, who set the pace for a tough guy in any movie. He's a classic American icon, who immigrated here but is still held as one of the greatest American movie stars and also served as governor of California.

Close behind him was Sylvester Stallone with all-time classics like Rocky and Rambo. You can't forget Clint Eastwood. Though not a huge, terminating, muscle-bound, soldier-style guy, he was depicted as the prototypical American tough guy. At eighty years old, he came out with a great movie, *Gran Torino,* classic to his style, which was ridiculed by modern media as racist and disrespectful. It's a movie—get over it, or don't watch it! Do you think that banning a movie that contains offensive vernacular will stop people from using it in real life? The above guys have stood the test of time, not only with their classic movies that youth still watch today, but with more recent movies like *Gran Torino*, the latest *Rambo*, and *Terminator 3*.

Who are the tough guys of today's Hollywood? Let's see, Ashton Kutcher in *The Guardian*, Tobey Maguire in *Spiderman*, and Matt Damon in the Bourne trilogy. While those are all good movies, I can't help but wonder, where has the big, tough American image gone? We have chosen a bunch of wimps to portray this generation's cinema heroes.

REALITY SHOWS

While on the subject, let's talk about today's "reality" shows. Everyone has seen them while surfing the channels. They are shows like *The Real World*, *Road Rules*, *What Not to Wear*, *Queer Eye for the Straight Guy*, and *America's Next Top Model*. First of all, none of these depict any version of the average American "reality." *Road Rules* and *The Real World* are a bunch of wannabe tough guys and drama queen girls who want a piece of fame. They compete in stupid games that my ten-year-old nephew could dominate, and they live together in some fancy apartment, having staged arguments. What is so interesting about this? Everyone involved in these shows is ridiculous. Stop wasting airtime and make something of your life. And for those who watch these shows, I don't even know what to say—find something better to do.

What Not to Wear? Are you serious, America? You really have that little to do that you would watch a show that is about fashion rules? If you watch this show, especially men, you need to grow up and get out more. For those of you who don't know what this show is, it's a gay man, or at least someone who acts like one, and a woman who gives money to someone they choose to "make over" or redo her wardrobe.

Then, at the end of the show, the made-over woman comes back home, and all her friends cheer her on about how good she looks. She usually cries and says how much more self-esteem the opportunity gave her, or some other sobbing load of garbage. I never knew there was that much *science* behind getting dressed: what colors go with what, what shoes match this, belt color, and whatever else they can come up with. I truly think this is a consumer trap to get people to invest in the clothing industry that has been damaged by the current economic state. When I hear a guy say "ew" about a girl's belt, it makes me want to puke. There is a time to dress up, but this show implies that you can't go out of your house without being a fashion icon.

Okay, the last one was bad, but *Queer Eye for the Straight Guy?* (Spike channel countered this with *Straight Plan for the Gay Man*, which was promptly taken off the air.) *Queer Eye* is a show in which some homo comes into a guy's house, throws out a bunch of his stuff, and makes his life more feminine. What true American guy would go along with that? I don't care how much my wife criticized me about my wardrobe (which she never would), I would never subject myself to some homosexual instructing me on fashion. Hey, if you want to look pretty, or whatever you call it, go ahead, but real men don't care if their shoes don't match their belt during regular day-to-day activity. Someone please explain to that guy that some men dress for functionality and comfort. I would like to see him push his car out of a ditch or change his tire in his Versace outfit. Again I ask, America, do you really have nothing better to do than sit around watching this junk? In the one episode I watched while I was doing research for this book, the queer came in the dude's house and threw all his clothes out the window. What would really have gotten your ratings up would have been if the dude had responded by throwing the gay guy out right behind them.

With *America's Next Top Model*, Tyra Banks turned in her runway shoes and started a show using her legacy as a model to stay in the spotlight. While this is truly brilliant, and my hat is off to her for capitalizing on the opportunity, you would think that she would actually pick hot chicks with natural beauty, rather

> What type of message are we sending to [young girls]—that if you starve yourself and look like a scarecrow, you are pretty?

than the busted-up, emaciated drama queens that actually make the cut. While not completely knocking you, Tyra, this show is ridiculous. You have a man addressed as "Miss Jay Alexander" in drag. What type of image and example are we setting for kids these days? And especially for the young girls of America who watch this show, what message are we sending to them—that if you starve yourself and look like a scarecrow, you are pretty?

It's the image that a show like this, and the whole modeling world, projects that encourages our teenage daughters have eating disorders. If a girl is five-foot-eight and weighs more than a hundred pounds, she thinks she is fat. Being able to count all your ribs in the mirror is disgusting. You want to look at the epitome of fit and healthy, look at decathletes. Tyra, the fact that you had to maintain an emaciated frame while modeling is the reason you can't keep the pounds off now. Do you really want to subject others to that type of unhealthy lifestyle? When these girls are cut from the show is the funniest part for me; they break down as if it were the end of the world. Look, lady, if you really want to succeed as a model, you don't need Tyra's blessing. Go out and do it on your own.

These types of shows are emasculating America. Depicting someone in drag to be successful and cool is crushing the image of America and eliminating the little strength left in today's youth. Other countries see these programs and laugh; so how does it reflect on us as a nation?

Also, with shows like this, Hollywood is making it seem as if men are supposed to be emotional and weak. Men are not usually sensitive by nature. While you need to be caring to be a good man, I don't think that men today should be frowned upon for not being emotional. If my wife asks me what I think of an outfit, I tell her the truth, and while she may be upset with me for a minute if I give negative feedback, she gets over it, and the night is that much better. If your wife or girlfriend asks you if you think she's gained weight, you should be able to tell her, "Yes, honey, you've gained about ten pounds" without her getting all mad at you if that is, in fact, the truth. I believe women only ask that question if they already know the answer. Ladies, if you think you have gotten fatter, and you ask your husband or boyfriend, and he answers you honestly, don't be mad. Wouldn't you rather he be honest than merely tell you what you want to hear?

THE GAY LIFE

Men of America, are you as curious as I am about when it became okay to be gay? I briefly addressed this earlier, but today more and more people are "coming out of the closet." Did I miss something? The human body is not designed for homosexuality. People think, *it's the twenty-first century. I am free to express myself in any way I want.* No, homosexuality is a disease and should be treated that way.

One hundred years ago, if you were gay, you made yourself straight, at least to the public. When it all boils down, we are still animals. Primordial instinct tells us to reproduce. Gays can't have babies, and that does not mean they should adopt them either. But from a scientific standpoint (which I know you liberals are all about), that means they have no purpose on this planet. While many gays out there may be nice people and assets to society, I still believe their ideology is not right. The mainstream media and our television networks are portraying all these things as acceptable, causing an epidemic.

This book is about true American values and how to uphold an honest country. Part of the reason I wrote this book was to bring public attention to things such as this. How can we do that if we have priests running around molesting little boys and people saying it's okay? These molesters are getting no punishments for ruining children's lives. We need to stand up and take back our country's dignity! Even given my own personal tragedy with this garbage, I stood up and fought back. We should all do the same.

THE ROLE OF MEN

In the previous chapter, I briefly discussed the woman's role in today's society. Now I would like to take a minute to talk about the man's role. Earlier in this chapter, I talked about male movie icons; now let's look at the common guy in a similar light. When I hang out with friends back home in Connecticut, they find it fascinating that I can handle a gun, know how to fight, can jumpstart a car, remodel a bathroom, and know how to cook a gourmet meal from an animal I killed three hours prior. Why is this so? This country was founded on men being the providers and protectors. Having these skills should be the norm, not an anomaly. While some aspects of that have changed in the provider category, men should still know how to do basic man things, such as hunt, cook, or jumpstart a car. While you don't have to do it for fun, you should know how, because you never know if you are going to need it.

Why doesn't someone start a show called *Man Skills* and just show things that men need to know how to do. You could put together a DVD series called *Manhood* or something like that. All you crazy networks out there, you could even make a reality show out of it. Find a responsible guy who works a nine-to-five job as a dockhand, police officer, or lumberjack and televise it. That way people can see that there is still hope for true *mankind.*

This is especially true for shooting a gun. You see, Democrats and liberals, teaching people how to use guns doesn't make them criminals and will only make them more knowledgeable, safe, and capable in the event they ever needed to use one. A serial killer is going to learn how to use that gun one way or another. Just think what it would be like if every man knew how to use a gun and was able to carry that gun and use it to defend his family or other innocent people. Imagine the different outcome of the Fort Hood shooting in Texas, if every one of those victims had been carrying a weapon; someone would have put him down.

Today, though, even the military doesn't allow personal guns on a military base, even with a valid state permit. Hmm, a federally funded organization is not obeying the Second Amendment? Sounds unjust to me. The mainstream media seized the chance to cram more gun-control measures down our throats. It was immediately televised as, "How did he get a gun?" and, "If guns were controlled, this wouldn't have happened." While not all men are the rugged type, they all should possess the knowledge of one. I see too many men today who can't wire a ceiling fan or gut a fish, and who don't even have calluses on their hands. Society's man is not what he should or used to be.

> People like that are real men . . . while you sit around getting a public relations degree.

The term *Renaissance man* is often used to describe a "real man" today. The public needs to realize that today's man is getting softer and softer. Much of this is due to modern society suppressing so much of the male instinct. It used to be that, if two guys had an argument, they would fight it out, and that was that. Now, if two guys get into a fight, there are assault charges and lawyer fees. Even if neither side chooses to press charges, they could still be charged with something like disturbing the peace. If that isn't enough, the media will smear them as barbarian or uncivilized. Few anchors out there respond positively to a story of a man knocking someone out deservedly or people hunting animals. Some even go so far as to alienate people in the military as warmongers, brutes, grunts, or right-wing extremists. But those are real men, who stand up and fight when time and country call for it, while you sit around getting a public relations degree.

BATTLE ON THE HOME FRONT

VIOLENCE WORKS

Contrary to popular belief, violence *does* solve problems. It should never be a first resort, but it works in the end. A case in point: war. The left has recently smeared the idea of war so badly that people have turned against the military and become ferocious towards George W. Bush for his policies in Iraq. Mankind has fought so many wars for so many reasons, and there is always a resolution at the end of the war. It may not be what everyone wanted, but it is always what the bigger, more powerful force wanted. It's almost like a more cut-and-dried version of a vote—majority rules. Michael Moore, if you have a better way of solving these types of conflicts, I'm all ears.

As for the rest of you antiwar wimps out there, I bet you would change your mind about war really fast if you didn't have it as good as you do now. In fact, if it weren't for America's superior power, we would all probably be speaking German and living under a dictator. Some of America's greatest icons have been war heroes. George Washington, Ulysses S. Grant, and Andrew Jackson were all great leaders in battle, and all are American political icons and heroes. It just seems that not enough people strive to live up to honor as our forefathers did.

THE MISINFORMING MEDIA

In addition to portraying the wrong kinds of heroes and idealizing immoral behavior, the media also controls the dissemination of information. The news media sways the people more than anything else. Unfortunately, most of the media today presents the opinions of the producers and reporters, rather than the facts. As a result, I believe the media does more harm than good.

For example, American perceptions of the War on Terror wouldn't be nearly as bad as they are today were it not for the media's skewed treatment of it. Liberal reporting on the war brought the country farther away from patriotism than ever before. And if you want to see something blown out of proportion, watch the news networks cover a story that can be construed as a human rights issue. I have seen the most ridiculous cases and stories scrutinized by media to the point of changing laws. It is not always bad, but if it stopped altogether, it would be worth the marginal loss of the few genuine, unbiased human rights stories the media present.

One of the rare good examples was when *The O'Reilly Factor* brought attention to Mark Hulett, the man who had repeatedly raped a child. He had originally been sentenced to a mere sixty days in prison and counseling until Bill O'Reilly aired the case, and Hulett eventually had his sentence extended from three to ten years. Normally the media works in the criminal's favor. It makes me sick to see how some of the issues are reported today.

The truth is, the public does *not* always have the right to know certain things. Examples are Guantanamo Bay (GITMO), the war in Iraq and Afghanistan, SEAL Team 6, and who's dating who in Hollywood. GITMO, if you missed it, despite how extensively it was covered in the news, is where America holds its Prisoners of War (POWs) and international criminals. The media is trying to get their hands on the pictures of the interrogation techniques and treatment of these guys. But what good could possibly come of that? They are going to create some sort of pity party for these criminals here in America and rally for their rights.

An example is when the blurry photos surfaced of what looked to be people being tortured. Without verification, the mainstream media raised a huge fuss, saying they were GITMO detainees being tortured. There were nationwide pity parties and outcries of civil rights until it was discovered that they were not prisoners of GITMO, but rather drunken college pledges. Remember, giving aid to these criminals and terrorists is an act of treason. But they are people and deserve their rights, too, people say. Rights? They gave up those rights when they knowingly waged an act of war against the United States or committed other serious crimes. The people in GITMO are criminals; they deserve to be there. If Al-Qaeda were to have you as their prisoner, you know what they would do? They would set up a video camera, saw your head off, and put it on YouTube so your family could watch—that's how *they* use the media.

If you really need to know what is going on in Iraq or Afghanistan, then join the military, pick up a gun, go over there, and witness it for yourself. Reporters going to Iraq and other war zones are an unnecessary annoyance and risk. Unless you are going to use your diplomacy stick (your gun) to make a difference, you don't belong there. Yes, there are innocent people suffering, but the local government doesn't care. So why should we spend valuable resources trying to convince them otherwise, after thousands of years of this practice? It's a losing battle. You want to donate money to them? Don't bother; give it to our country's needs instead. The Iraqi government can't and won't support itself, so with America gone, those people will probably go back to how they have been living for the last three thousand years.

Do you want to know what was really going on over there? Americans were dying because they were too scared of being thrown in jail for murder if they inadvertently engaged an Iraqi civilian. There was no progress, and when America left that dump, Al-Qaeda or local militias began taking it back. The government will eventually be overthrown, and those not on board with radical Islamic ideology will be killed. There you have it, America; I saved you an hour of watching the news that you can now fill with something productive.

Another example of craziness in the media is that they report and respect stuff like Janet Napolitano's homeland security speech in 2009, in which there was no mention of terrorists or Al-Qaeda at all. All she talked about was FEMA and hurricanes. Stuff like this should not even be aired. It benefits no one and does not boost ratings. Besides, no one cares about what she has to say, because she [Janet Napolitano] is probably the person most detached from reality.

The same goes for Nancy Pelosi's right-wing extremist speech. Thank God that most people were outraged enough about it for her to get some negative publicity from it. Or how about when the public was demanding to know what was in the health care bill, and she responded, "We have to pass the bill first to see what's in it," and the mainstream media still praised her. Some transparency. Hey, Media, you want something to do? Send your paparazzi to follow her and reveal to the public what an idiot she really is. I'm sure everyone remembers when she asked for their health care votes, even if it cost them their careers, which, for a large number of them, it did. Isn't forcing through a bill that you know the public doesn't want the opposite of serving the people? And if this bill is so great, why is her own health care plan different than what's described in the bill?

While we are on the paparazzi topic, I want to talk about how people have made a living on what shoes Tom Cruise wore yesterday. You people are the bottom of the barrel. Leave them alone. You are reinforcing the problem of giving these actors political power by giving them publicity. Actors are essentially glorified Xboxes—they entertain people, and that is all. If my Xbox gave me political advice, I would take it with the same skepticism with which I do an actor's. Put that in your pipe and smoke it, Alec Baldwin.

Remember when Paul McCartney visited the White House to play a private concert for Obama and said, "After the last eight years, it's great to have a president who knows what a library is"? He then refused to apologize for it, even after he was informed that former first lady, Laura Bush, led a massive campaign for children's literacy, and good ol' George and Dick read more than a combined one hundred books a year. Well, who's the jerk now, Sir Paul? Quit spouting off about politics and sing.

I also can't stand to see those stupid who's-fat-and-who's-not tabloid covers. I really don't care if Paris Hilton got another ticket for driving under the influence (DUI). These are such miniscule points in today's society. Tabloids, you are taking people's interest away from important things that need our focus. Report something useful!

BATTLE ON THE HOME FRONT

FACTS OR FICTION?

In a recent poll by the mainstream media, seven out of ten media icons admittedly lean to the left. That's interesting, because for so long I thought that was the case and never had any proof of it. It was proven in the coverage of both candidates for the Massachusetts senate election. MSNBC and CNN covered the candidates almost 70–30 Democrat versus Republican, while Fox News covered them evenly. That's huge when it comes to reporting certain issues. The mainstream media has the tendency to put their own little spin on things. I also have seen the radical left make things up to support their cases when they had no actual evidence (e.g., global warming). When called on it, they just ignore the facts or use a phrase such as "undeniable evidence" or "radical climate change" without actually producing any evidence, and then they quickly change the subject.

The whole progressive party is changing, distorting, and erasing history. Our forty-fourth president is really dividing this country by using the media. He campaigned on transparency, which got the mainstream media on his side. Then he used that leverage to mold his zombielike followers to do what he wanted. Now, he is trying to silence and discredit Fox News for telling us the truth about him and his policies. He is trying to control free speech in America. Sound familiar? Woodrow Wilson imprisoned people for speaking out against the war or his views, and I don't think Obama is far from that kind of thinking. The First Amendment sucks when it's not working in your favor, huh?

President Obama is trying to silence any opposition to his "reform" of this country. He has gone so far as to try to control the Internet. At a graduation speech at Hampton University, he said in reference to media devices and materials, "Information becomes a distraction." No, sir. Just as former U.N. Secretary General, Kofi Annan said, "Knowledge is power. Information is liberating. Education is the premise of progress, in every society, in every family." If that's the case, why is President Obama's cabinet trying to limit and even control information? President Obama knows that, if people are presented with the facts, it will discredit his standpoint and values.

In 1917, President Wilson created the Committee on Public Information. He allegedly cut the flow of information to noncompliant news agencies, which meant networks that presented the facts as they *were* and not as he *wanted* them to be. Does everyone remember the fuss Obama made over Glenn Beck, even going so far as to say, "We need to take care of the Glenn Beck problem"? Problem? I'm pretty sure he presents the facts as is and holds true to core values, such as faith, hope, and charity. And yes, I guess that makes him a problem for this administration. The president even went so far as to accuse Beck of "sedition." Sedition is what people are charged with who commit treason, and the president wanted to accuse someone with it who publicly cries over the trampling of the Constitution. I mean, come on, Bush never accused MSNBC of sedition; he took his licks from them and moved on.

Some other members of President Obama's cabinet think that we need to take conservative views out of the media as well. This is the beauty of free speech and a free press. You can say whatever you want, and if someone doesn't like it, then they should just ignore it. Imagine if the tables were turned; how would the progressives like it if we shut down MSNBC for not agreeing with the conservative movement and the Tea Party?

BLOCKING THIS BOOK

In a similar light, I have had to jump through hoops, so to speak, in order to get this book published while on active duty. It seemed that, no matter who I called, they always had nothing to do with the approval process, and there was somewhere or someone else for me to send the manuscript for "review." Following suit with the administration, the military is a dictatorship and did not want this book to come out, nor did they want to be associated with its content. That was vividly displayed by the different departments dragging their feet during the approval process. It took months to even get an email back about who to contact for different reviews. I had to have a lawyer send a letter to my chain of command, pressuring them to give me a response. Funny that within a few days of that letter being sent, I received an email from the Judge Advocate General (JAG) at my command, saying they had completed the review of my manuscript and gave me all the needed direction from there.

> The military is a dictatorship and did not want this book to come out, nor did they want to be associated with its content.

By that point, I had given up on my chain of command and had already given the rights to the book to a limited liability company (LLC) formed by a family friend. I advised him to do whatever he wants with it so I would have no legal connection to the publication. It took months with no results, and suddenly there was a letter from a lawyer on the JAG's desk, and he miraculously found the time to do his job. Well, America, you be the judge. There is fact and truth in this book, but many people in control are very hesitant to let someone call them on their mistakes.

MALIGNED BY THE MEDIA

I have seen good things portrayed with good reporting, but there is always someone who finds the negative in it. For example, the Bush administration did so many things wrong in the media's eyes. I had the opportunity to meet with this American hero very briefly and also listen to a lot of his reasoning, and his quote was, "Every decision I have made has been based on how to protect the homeland." I don't understand why the media smeared so much of his work. Maybe, if CNN had endured a rocket attack on their headquarters, their eyes might have been opened, but that didn't happen, because President Bush and his policies did such a good job on meeting their goal.

Another thing that makes me really angry is that President Bush endured personal attacks on everything he did, while Obama can go out and eat out all over town, order more catering than any other president, play basketball, reserve the entire Taj Mahal for a conference, and go on multiple vacations a year while in the middle of a financial crisis, and he was praised by the media. Doesn't anyone think he has more important things to do? This is another example of the biased reporting that riddles the networks.

While conducting some training in Florida in 2006, I had the opportunity to meet with "Mack," another former Navy SEAL from the Discovery Channel show *Future Weapons*. Of course, he was there with his entire camera crew and PR people to attend one of our training scenarios for his show. After we had finished our brief, I was approached by his PR representative and her notepad. Knowing that I was about to be quoted on everything I said, I tried to keep my composure. That didn't last long.

Her first question was, "So what do you think about the media in Iraq?"

"They have no business being there," I said with a cold tone.

"Why, don't you think America has a right to know?" she responded, as she adjusted into a defensive, crossed-armed posture.

"Nope. If they want to know, they should pick up a gun and join the ranks."

"Ha, you know you guys wouldn't be making nearly as much progress as you are without the support of the media. We are helping America win this war," she snapped in a rude tone.

"Look, lady, I don't know where you get your facts, but the media does nothing but get in the way. All they are is a bunch of know-it-alls like you, messing up stories and defending the terrorists over there. You and people like you generated the 'baby-killer' reputation with regard to American soldiers. Get a real job, lady."

I was so hacked off I had to walk away. I should have paid more attention to the culture warrior's strategy: keep your cool, no matter what, and they will eventually trip themselves up. The battle was hers, Mr. O'Reilly, but I counted it a partial victory when Mack took her notebook and gave it to my officer.

You see, this is the general attitude of, and my problem with, the media: they think they know everything and that, in some way, they are morally right for doing what they are doing. And most of them are vultures, who will lie, cheat, or steal to get the story they want.

The Moronic Media

During Hurricane Irene in 2011, there was a reporter on the beach in seventy mile per hour winds, reporting on the storm. While he was out there, he was telling people that they needed to "get in their homes" and "there is no room for people to be playing around out here. It would be foolish for anyone to stay out here." As a few people walked and drove by during the course of his broadcast, he called them "stupid" for being outdoors in a hurricane because they could get injured and emergency crews would have to rescue them, putting more lives at risk. Naturally, everyone in the studio agreed with him, and they had a thirty-second conversation about how stupid those people were for being on the beach. Hey Moron, you are on the beach just like the idiots you were describing. You get off the beach as well!

Another thing that is ridiculous about the media is that, if there is nothing else to report for the day, they bring on a new anchor to talk about the same issue with essentially the same vantage point. Very seldom does a new reporter shed new light on an already covered topic. They will harp on small issues and make them bigger controversies than they truly are.

Television engages people's emotions more than radio or newspapers, so sometimes media will try to guilt America into things, such as helping little kids in Africa for a dollar a day. We've all seen these commercials, with some poor kid suffering, with ribs sticking out and a cleft lip. Naturally, you feel bad and want to help the kid, as I often do when I see these things. But it's not fair or sensible for the media to show things like that. I know it seems harsh, but let's worry about the problems in our country first, and then we'll feed the rest of the world. I'm all for charity, but genocide and starvation have been going on all over the world for as long as man has walked upright. Stuff like that is going to happen, no matter what is aired on TV, so save your ad time for something that is more pertinent, and I don't mean taxpayer-funded census commercials during the Super Bowl. Yeah, that also happened.

While there are some good reporters out there, these media machines should take a step back and think about whether each story is really worth reporting, or if they are just aiming for higher ratings. Fox News reports honestly and conservatively, and that is why they have been the number one news network for several years.

SIX

Entitlement

One of the root problems with America's progressively collapsing society and economy is the large number of people who feel the government owes them something. It's this level of entitlement that we need to suppress in order to rebuild a more successful society. Examples are welfare, pampered children, and the general acceptance and reward of those who do poor or mediocre work. Just as in the recent debt debate, the president fought hard to defend all of the entitlement programs despite the fact that we cannot afford to sustain them. At what point did it start paying off to not work hard? George Washington is rolling over in his grave.

While I have spent much of this book defending our government, I believe this problem is derived from a strong government in the first place. The problem is that the government, Republican or Democrat recently, doesn't know when to stop giving. Republicans talk about cutting these programs but never actually do, and Democrats just want to give everything to everyone, except the "greedy Wall Street executives."

Battle on the Home Front

Government Handouts

Every year the government shells out hundreds of billions of dollars in welfare alone. I believe some of the entitlement programs are very necessary, such as Social Security that you pay into your whole life, and certain aspects of Medicare. But others are not only ridiculous, they perpetuate the cycle of more spending down the road. For instance, if you have no job or an underpaying job, you can file for unemployment, general welfare, or Medicaid. Many people take these handouts and never aspire to be anything more or intend to give anything back. Even worse, typically these are the people who claim that they have it so bad and cry about not getting more or their benefits are running out. It's also funny that the crime rate among this economic class of people is statistically higher as well.

Basically, people who leach off the government still complain about it, and as if handouts aren't enough, they still go and break the laws put into place by the system that is supporting them. What happened to not biting the hand that feeds you? The bottom line is that nothing is perfect, and if you fall down, these systems are there to help pick you up, but they are not meant to be a permanent answer to your failures. Grow up, take responsibility, and get a job.

A simple solution to all this would be to cut welfare altogether. If people can't support themselves or their children, guess what? Tough luck; natural selection, I guess. There are more than enough opportunities out there to get a job or succeed financially in one way or another. It's even more so if you put in a little extra effort and spend one day at the library (also a free service brought to you by your government). You can start your own business and make your own job and many more for others too. This is called "contributing to society." Some people are just too lazy, and they know that if they just sit around blaming everything on others, eventually someone will throw them a bone.

I know that last section seems a little bit harsh, but it is no harsher than the effects of this lazy idealism, which was handed down to my generation by the previous one's success and hard work. So many people my parents' age worked very hard, because it was instilled in them that, "You reap what you sow." Recently, kids have been growing up with the idea that what they need and want will always — be provided. I know a bunch of people from high school who work dead-end jobs and take one — class in a community college, if any. They live with their parents, mooching off them with no intention of ever getting out on their own, and some of them are nearing thirty years old. Get a grip, parents! Kick your kids out, and make them cut it on their own. Kicking them out and forcing them to grow up is only part of parenting and does not mean you don't love them. You are doing more harm by letting them ride the system. All you who have seen the movie *Stepbrothers* know that, while hilarious and a little farfetched, it depicts a common theme in some of today's youth.

BAILOUTS AND BOGUS PROPOSALS

In the recent years of this economic downfall, there have been many ridiculous proposals. For instance, now if you miss or are late on a mortgage payment, you are more likely to get help from the government and the bank than you are if you are a responsible American and pay it on time every time. Apparently, we've learned nothing from the fact that the housing market is a big part of why we fell into a recession in 2008. People got mortgages they couldn't afford in the first place. Now they feel they are entitled to be bailed out by the government for their own mistakes. You can't necessarily blame them, though, since all the banks, which made the same mistake on a larger scale, are getting billions of dollars to stay afloat. This bailout from both Bush and Obama was the worst idea ever.

Looking back on history, which you would think leaders of this country would do, Glenn Beck has repeatedly discussed how Wilson raised taxes to over 70 percent in some brackets, dropped credit requirements, and printed more money in order to pull the country out of a depression. What happened? It got worse!

Then, in 1921, President Warren Harding, though he was eventually corrupted by his power, did the opposite by cutting taxes in half and terminating any federal bailouts then in place. In his shortened term in office, he cut unemployment by half, and the economy turned around in less than eighteen months, which led to the economic boom of the twenties. But that's just historical fact; remember, Obama knows better than that.

Americans are entitled to a better country and better leadership. The unemployment rate in 2011 was still above 9 percent, despite the "foolproof" bailout program, and major companies are still making employee cutbacks (and not just because they can't afford the new health care law). What did the bailouts solve besides a few trillion more on the national deficit? They created the belief that, if major banks and companies get into trouble, the government will bail them out. And they launched the idea that, if you work hard and pay your bills on time, you will not get any help from your government. According to Nancy Pelosi, though, the bailouts from her reign of terror single-handedly stopped the unemployment rate from exceeding 16 percent. Where do they get these numbers anyway? I would like to see one shred of evidence that points that way. Democrats, no one can prove either way, but what can be proven is that the unemployment rate surely didn't go down.

My wife and I applied for Obama's mortgage assistance program. A Wells Fargo employee told us that we were unlikely to receive any assistance. Why? It was because we had never missed a payment and because our house is worth seventy-five thousand dollars less than when we bought it six years ago, making it an upside-down mortgage.

We then tried to refinance our house to a lower rate, but without an additional twenty-five thousand dollars to put down on top of the fifty thousand dollars we'd already put down, we could not refinance, due to the current market. So, pretty much because we did the responsible thing, and the banks knew we would not walk away from our mortgage, they denied us any assistance. Hey, morons, that is the very reason you should be helping people like me. In keeping with the American way, though, I decided that I am responsible for a debt that I promised to pay and started Tarzan Tree Service in Virginia Beach in order to supplement my income and live a little more comfortably.

Let's clarify this: my property value tanks while I still continue to make full, on-time payments on a principal that is more than my house is currently worth. Meanwhile, banks and financial institutions, you are receiving billions of dollars to keep your heads above water after borrowing or loaning too much money to people with risky credit, but you won't adjust my interest rate. We had over fifty thousand dollars of equity from the down payment on our house, which has now vanished into thin air. Hey, major banks, you got free money—help out your loyal customers too. Are there any logical people left out there? Oh, that's right, it would cut into your year-end bonus. People like my wife and me are the good guys—you should want to keep us happy, because we keep you in business. Wow! Most of those executives went to business school?

> Entering this bail-out phase brings us dangerously close to the line of socialism.

This sends the wrong message. It tells people that, if you are irresponsible and can't make the cut, the government will pick up the slack. This unearned government assistance is killing us these days. I know this will come as a shock to many, but if you want to live a prosperous life, then you have to work for it. Entering this bailout phase brings us dangerously close to the line of socialism.

WELFARE AND UNEMPLOYMENT

Along these lines are welfare and unemployment allowances. I know of people who don't get a new job and just collect unemployment until the month or two before it runs out. Then they get on their horses and find jobs, because it is just easier. Congratulations, you're a bum. And believe me, I say it right to your face. This is ridiculous! Uncle Sam should come to your house, slap you in the face, and take the food right out of your refrigerator. As for the government, we wouldn't have nearly as many financial problems if you would stop shelling out hundreds of billions of dollars each year for these lazy parasites.

I know what you are thinking: *the government has given it to people for so long, some people wouldn't know how to live without it. So many people would suffer and endure hardships without it.* Guess what. Hardship and suffering breed motivation, and the people who don't rise to the occasion will be filtered out. Call it natural selection again, if you will. After a decade or two of people griping, most of the people you don't want in a society anyway either won't be there or will find a sense of responsibility. There would be an initial outcry, but fortunately the hard workers outnumber the bums, so through sheer numbers the useless members of society would be overcome. Besides, generally the people who are receiving substantial government assistance are in that position because they are too lazy to do anything for themselves in the first place. So they would yell about it for a little while but never take any action. Rest assured, the American Civil Liberties Union (ACLU) and other civil rights organizations would do everything in their power to counter this, up to and probably including filing a lawsuit against the government for not giving people money. Sound crazy? They've done worse.

ENTITLEMENT

EQUAL OPPORTUNITY

While we are fixing this glitch, we should also yank the rug out from under these equal-opportunity, pot-smoking activists and give them no credibility in America's courtrooms. Lyndon B. Johnson, the thirty-sixth president, should have been slapped in the face when he put this insane system into effect, but he wasn't. Now it falls to us to fix it. Times were different, and there was some need for government interventions while racism was still legitimately holding people back, but that time is over—we elected a half-black president for pity sake.

I equate this system with childhood and the end of a parenting role. When a child is growing up, the parents hold the child's hand while he's learning to walk, help him swing a baseball bat, and sit in the passenger seat while he's taught how to drive, much as we have done for the last seventy years. Once the individual is grown (like America is now), the parent steps back and gives less and less assistance until eventually exiting the mentoring role. This country has held people's hands and taught them everything that can be taught, and all people do is whine about not getting more. It's time for the government to take their hand out of people's lives and focus on the big picture of a functioning country and not individuals. It's no longer Uncle Sam's job to put food on your plate. It is your job now to raise yourselves and your children. And this can be done merely by going back to what this country was founded on—hard work.

CRIMINAL RIGHTS

Another issue of entitlement is criminal rights. There are differing levels of criminality. Someone who is convicted of reckless driving is much different than a child abuser or murderer. With this in mind, why are these major criminals still entitled to such pampering in prison? Put them to work; throw them in a mine, and make them break rocks all day, as North Korea would do. Once you are convicted of a serious crime, you should no longer be entitled to luxuries. If you choose to live outside society by breaking these laws, you should no longer be entitled to the same rights as everyone else. If you are a convicted sex offender, and you get beat up by some angry law-abiding citizen as a result of it, then you should not have the right to charge that person with assault. You did it to someone else, so why is it not okay when it happens to you? You think because you did some time in prison that all sins are forgiven? No one is that divine here on earth, pal. You are still a dirtbag and should consequently be reminded of that for the rest of your life. Your victim has to live with it; why shouldn't you? The same goes for murderers and other violent criminals.

I think the judicial system is too lax as it is. You kill, you should be killed, immediately, and not spend nine years wasting tax dollars on death row. Yes, there are flaws in every system, and an innocent person might suffer sometime, but that is the price of a better system. I don't see how people think the death penalty is wrong. Texas has it all figured out; good for them. The common argument is, "Who is the government to end someone's life?" Well, I ask, "What makes you so divine that you think these criminals should be forgiven?" Most people support the government when it comes to getting personal justice, but some get wobbly-kneed and hesitant when it comes to seeing that criminals get theirs.

What's even more insufferable is that these criminals receive far more than they should while serving a prison sentence. Criminals are treated with respect by the guards, have three square meals a day, and are given better medical care than half the law-abiding citizens of the country. Criminals have no ground to complain about rights, whether they are violated or not. Have you ever seen Third World countries and their prisons? I have. They get food sometimes; they receive no medical treatment; and they are beaten until they die, if the guards feel they have had enough, or they give up the information that is desired. I'm not saying that this method is civil, but it really illustrates the point that, if you commit a crime, you will get punished. Our judicial system does not punish criminals accordingly in this country.

This personal experience really illustrates the ridiculousness of our judicial system. While working with my tree company along some railroad tracks in Norfolk, Virginia, we witnessed someone who appeared to be dumping debris along the tracks. As my business partner and I approached him, he immediately left. We informed the homeowner and continued with the job. Months later, I received a court summons, ordering my presence at 9:00 a.m. in the city criminal court regarding that case. I sat through countless cases in which predominantly black males, dressed in sagged sweatpants and tank tops, cursed out the judge and displayed constant levels of disrespect to the standing officers. Finally, around 1:00 p.m., we were called to the bench to testify. After all seven of us were individually interviewed as witnesses, we were corralled into the hallway for another hour while the judge deliberated the sentence. The prosecutor eventually came into the hall and said the defendant was found guilty, he would have to pay a one-thousand-dollar fine, and we could all go home.

I was shocked! The court system had subpoenaed three neighbors, who I'm sure were less than thrilled to be there; two police officers, who cost the city overtime pay for four hours each; and my business partner and me, who had to cancel a full day's work, which usually totals over two thousand dollars. And their verdict was only a one-thousand-dollar fine. Does no one see anything wrong with this stupidity? And that doesn't include all the hours the city attorney's office had to spend to prepare for the case. My company sent the city a bill for the five-dollar parking garage fee and man-hours we lost, but we have yet to receive a check or even a response.

Our legal system is flawed by compassion for criminals. Are all criminals entitled to fair trials? Yes, I believe they are, and that is their right, as endowed by our Creator, but there are possible factors involved in modern law that can make having a fair trial a headache. What I don't understand is, why can a murderer submit a plea bargain, admit guilt, and receive a lesser sentence for the same crime? You're either guilty or not; there should be no debating, no first or second degree. The sentence should stand. I know I am not a lawyer and may not understand all aspects of modern law, but I have read story after story of people having their houses broken into, and when they respond accordingly, they are put on trial for some wrongdoing. Any response to a situation like that should be justified. When six punks broke into my house, their lawyer was going to try to spin it around on me and charge me with excessive force. Are you serious? I am entitled to defend my own property. It is cases like that which take the focus off the real issue at hand and ultimately make it harder for good people to protect themselves and their families.

Rights for Enemies?

And what about the prisoners at GITMO? Those are not even Americans. They are people who have committed some sort of serious war crime against America or her citizens, and there are government officials there who think those people should be entitled to the same constitutionally protected rights as Americans? These prisoners have more rights than many of the American soldiers who captured them, because they get sympathy from organizations such as the ACLU that also happens to fund high-dollar lawyers for those heathens. Can you believe that there are Americans out there who are actually advocating the "rights" of our enemies?

I believe that is treason in itself, by letter of the law, so have a nice day, go join them at GITMO. You have to wonder if those idiots who want to release or give fair trials to war criminals realize that if they are able to get them out of prison and back to wherever they came from, they are going to go right back to what they were doing that landed them in prison. There is no lesson learning, rationalism, or rehabilitation for radical Muslims. They were willing to die for their cause. So do you think they give a rip about what some group therapy session has to offer them? Next time they strike, it could be at you, so stop defending them, and leave them there to rot. They are not entitled to anything, and no one holds enough moral high ground to think otherwise.

Sometimes I ask myself, *are we fighting a war against terror or not? Didn't Islamic people start it on September 11, 2001? Weren't Americans brutally murdered that day in Manhattan, Washington, and Pennsylvania? Why are we trying to win the hearts and minds of the Iraqis and Afghanis at the cost of more American lives? And why do we care about their infrastructure? Let's fight to win.*

Why am I supposed to care if a copy of the Quran was "desecrated" when an overworked American soldier kicked it or got it wet? I don't care; in fact, I couldn't care less. I'll care about the Quran when the fanatics in the Middle East start caring about the Holy Bible or maybe stop practicing sharia law. Maybe I'll care when these thugs tell the world they are sorry for chopping off Nick Berg's head while he screamed through his gurgling slashed throat. I might care when the cowardly insurgents in Iraq come out and fight like men, instead of disrespecting their own religion by hiding in mosques and sending their kids out in suicide vests.

When I hear a story about a soldier or intelligence agent roughing up an Iraqi terrorist to obtain information, not only do I not care, I sleep better. When I hear that a prisoner, who was issued a Quran and a prayer mat, and fed food that is paid for by my tax dollars, is complaining that his holy book is being mishandled, I think, *you've got to be kidding me.* Americans are upset because a solider disrespects an enemy of democracy?

As the saying goes, "Only two defining forces have ever offered to die for you: the first was Jesus Christ, and the other is the American GI. One died for your soul; the other for your freedom." So let's not give aid or support to the people who kill and condemn both of them.

We have grown too accustomed to giving people rights for just about any reason. Why in the world would you want to give more rights to someone who opposes everything for which you and your country stand? Most of these criminals now know that they have it better in our prisons than they do in their own country while free, and they can still practice their faith, which in their ideology is the only reason for living anyway. Those individuals are actually playing us against ourselves and our laws; yet we still have Americans complaining about their not having rights. Woe to you when that same person, whose rights you demanded, commits another crime, and this time it's against someone close to you. Blame yourself and no one else, because it is you and your assistance that gave him books in prison to teach him skills, a Quran and a prayer mat to strengthen his faith, and three meals a day to make him stronger and healthier. Can you look at yourself in the mirror and live with that? I couldn't.

At the same time, we are depriving our own citizens—in this case, our soldiers—of their rights. You would think they are entitled to more rights than these criminals. As it was covered so well in the media, I'm sure everyone heard about the SEALs who captured a high-value criminal in Iraq in September 2009. He had killed four American Blackwater contractors, dragged them through the streets, and hung their charred bodies from a bridge in Fallujah in March of 2004. I was one of the SEALs on the ground involved in the operation and as a witness in the trial. Having been on the mission and returned to the base where the complaint of abuse took place, I can say with the utmost certainty that no one touched, let alone abused, that detainee. He had a gun on target when we kicked in his door. It would have been well within the rules of engagement to shoot him.

And yet, three of my good friends were tried for the alleged abuse of that terrorist without any evidence to support their prosecution. Where was the chain of command during that, you ask? They are too worried about their bronze stars at the end of deployment to stand up for the men who delivered the results to make them eligible for it. That is a disgrace! Not only was a general not supporting us, he had publicly stated that he was disappointed in us for trying to cover it up, with not a shred of evidence to support his assertion. The three men who stood trial are the same heroes who make valuable headway in wars like this. These young men are the people deserving rights, protection, and support. America's loyalties are skewed and need to be put in check.

The Health Care Bill

Lastly is the topic of the health care bill that was recently signed into law and then ruled unconstitutional by a federal judge in Florida. People such as our nearly incompetent leaders on the left say that everyone is entitled to health care. No, we're not! Health care, like most things, is a luxury. If you work hard, you can buy your own, but it is not the responsibility of those who do work to make sure that those who don't work get proper medical care. Here is a letter to the president posted on Facebook and written by Dr. Roger Starner Jones, one of the many doctors out there who is angry about the new bill.

Dear Mr. President:

During my shift in the emergency room last night, I had the pleasure of evaluating a patient whose smile revealed an expensive shiny-gold tooth, whose body was adorned with a wide assortment of elaborate and costly tattoos, who wore a very expensive brand of tennis shoes, and who chatted on a new cellular telephone equipped with a popular R&B ringtone.

While glancing over her patient chart, I happened to notice that her payer status was listed as "Medicaid!" During my examination of her, the patient informed me that she smokes more than one pack of cigarettes every day, eats only at fast-food take-outs, and somehow still has money to buy pretzels and beer. And you and our Congress expect me to pay for this woman's health care? I contend that our nation's "health care crisis" is not the result of a shortage of quality hospitals, doctors, or nurses. Rather, it is the result of a "crisis of culture," a culture in which it is perfectly acceptable to spend money on luxuries and vices while refusing to take care of one's self or, heaven forbid, purchase health insurance. It is a culture based in the irresponsible credo that "I can do whatever I want to, because someone else will always take care of me." Once you fix this "culture crisis" that rewards irresponsibility and dependency, you'll be amazed at how quickly our nation's health care difficulties will disappear.

Respectfully,

Roger Starner Jones, MD

My wife is just entering the nursing field, and she sees many people who share this man's frustrations. If you hand out free care to people, it will only hurt the hardworking people of America.

Work hard and prosper; don't expect someone to give you a handout. Mark my words, if we continue down this path of entitlement, we will inevitably meet our demise. This babysitting is only made possible by those who do work hard and don't just take. One day enough people may get tired of paying for everyone else and decide to start collecting; it is unsustainable.

SEVEN

Government, Laws, and Loopholes

Today's government has become a circus compared to what it was originally intended. As I have said before, how can you serve as a politician, if you have never served in the military or civil service? You should not be allowed to make laws, if you have never put yourself on the line to uphold them. And how can you justifiably stand there, as Obama did, and award a soldier our highest medal for valor, having never served yourself?

There are so many government officials who talk so tough in their safe offices but would never pick up a gun to fight for their cause. Nancy Pelosi, can you look me in the eye and honestly say that, even if this country were completely the way you wanted it to be, you would pick up a gun and defend it? Everyone knows the answer to that. One of the most outspoken and opinionated people in modern politics, she would not even be willing to fight for her perfect country—shows her true loyalties.

If someone does not believe in fighting, that probably means he or she has never had to fight for anything. Anyone who reads this is welcome to challenge me on that. Some of our laws and rights that have been adhered to for as long as this country has been around are written in a vernacular different than that used today. Many people have tried to derive new meaning from these old laws to support their ideas. Somehow, they are often allowed to do that. As I mentioned earlier, just because you can't take people's guns away doesn't mean you should make it virtually impossible to obtain permits to legally possess firearms or the ammunition for them. Someone up there needs to recognize this and quickly. National Rifle Association (NRA), Tea Party, and like-minded true American organizations, keep up the good work. America appreciates it more than you know.

THE LAW

Laws are set in place for a reason. While there are occasionally acceptable caveats to the cut-and-dried laws, for the most part, these laws need to be followed to the T—by *everyone*. Assemblies larger and more invested than you and I have set those laws in place. If you don't agree with them, sorry about that—if you don't like it, either deal with it or leave. There will always be something that someone doesn't like about anything. So laws are created in the interest of safety, order, and in most cases, morality, not what will make everyone happy.

> This heinous organization thinks that it is okay for men to have sex with little boys and to have little crushes on them.

Unfortunately, some of these laws protect the wrong people and organizations, but that is another compromise that must be made for the values we have as a country. Organizations like the North America Man Boy Love Association (NAMBLA) are a disgrace. There have been numerous cases of child abuse in which the perpetrator has admitted to getting information from this organization and through similar reading material.

For those of you who don't know, this heinous organization thinks that it is okay for men to have sex with little boys and to have little crushes on them.

I have eleven nieces and nephews. If a man or woman touched one of them sexually or any other way that made them uncomfortable, there is no measure to the pain I would bring upon them. As discussed earlier, the Mark Hulett case in January 2006 provides an excellent example.

In Vermont, thirty-four-year-old Mark Hulett was sentenced to sixty days in prison for having repeated sexual contact with a girl, beginning when she was six, over a four-year period. Judge Edward Cashman said he made the sentence so short so Hulett could begin his rehabilitation when he got out of prison. Seeing how the minimum sentence for this offense was three years, it fortunately received national attention. Sixty days and rehab? Are you kidding me? This guy consciously and repeatedly committed a vulgar crime, and the state is interested in paying to "rehabilitate him." His sentence was merely a fraction of the length of time during which he repeatedly committed the crime. This guy should spend life behind bars at the least. If someone is demented enough to commit such a crime repeatedly over a four-year period, then there is probably little to no hope of rehabilitation.

Hulett sympathizers, what if it happened to your child, and the man who did it was back on the streets in less than two months? Would that be proper justice in your eyes? Moreover, would you feel safe in your justice system? My point is that morals need to be more heavily weighed into modern sentencing. After all, those are the morals on which our justice system was founded. I don't care what justification was given during his hearing; that man has forfeited all rights as a citizen.

MISLEADING OUR YOUTH

Another thing I read about while expanding my horizons to write this book was an incident at Boulder High School on April 10, 2007. There was a school-sanctioned assembly held by the principal and four other adults, who actively encouraged the students to use the drug ecstasy, smoke marijuana, have sex with multiple people, and have homosexual experiences. Joel Becker, a clinical psychologist attending, said, "I'm going to encourage you to have sex, and I'm going to encourage you to use drugs appropriately. And why I'm going to take that position is because you're going to do it anyway. So, my approach to this is to be realistic."

Negative! Those kids will not "do it anyway"; some will try it, some will dive headfirst into it, and some will do the right thing. If you encourage them, they will start thinking it is okay, and then there will an epidemic of drugged-up, homo nymphomaniacs out there. That is allowed? How did we get reduced to this much open antiestablishment nonsense? Those adults should have been punished, not praised as they were by some of their fellow townsfolk. If my kids went to that school, I would pull them out faster than a fat kid in dodge ball. Since most kids that age are on the fence about what kind of new things to experiment with in life, that is just swaying them in the wrong direction.

If the child of one of those speakers died from an overdose of ecstasy or contracted a sexually transmitted disease (STD), I'm sure somehow these same people would then blame it on someone else. It would be the government's fault for not educating the kids on how to do it safely, or some garbage like that. You may laugh and think I'm joking, but I am as serious as a heart attack. Instances like this have happened before. If something goes well for the progressives, it was by their own single hand that it worked; if it goes south, then it's inevitably someone else's fault.

BLUE LAWS

Though this may run a bit contrary to my previous statement regarding the necessity of obeying laws, there are many laws that are ridiculous and outdated and need to be removed. These are referred to as "blue laws," the just plain ridiculous laws that were put in place for no apparent reason. Blue laws mostly pertain to certain activities on Sundays, such as the purchase of alcohol and other useless restrictions. The state currently spends much more each year prohibiting or prosecuting people for these laws than it would cost to eradicate them once and for all. They should never have made it into the books in the first place. City officials, if you are not trying to fix things like this, then you are just as bad as the morons who wrote them.

POLITICIANS AND THE LAW

Despite all the laws that are out there, with a properly funded lawyer you can get yourself out of almost any crime today. Just look at O. J. Simpson or Casey Anthony. With faulty interpretations of the evidence, corrupt jurors, and enough media support, the system will buckle. Look at Charlie Rangel. Despite all the charges against him, he is still in office. Now more than ever, there are people slipping through the cracks and getting away with murder, literally. Depending on your celebrity status, you are sometimes even above the law.

> I guess it is easy to make crazy laws, if you don't have to abide by them.

Using our current president as an example again, everyone around him was being investigated in the lead-up to the election for some sort of discrimination or corruption. Why did no one think to take a deeper look at him? There was video proof of his supporting a certain reverend, who bashed whites. When it hit the media, he denied ever having any affiliation with the pastor, even though they had it on video. Like zombies, people just agreed, and no further investigation was conducted. And then came the real kicker—he was elected!

Why is that? President Obama is not the only one guilty of this. Politicians, blue and red, do things every day to warrant some sort of punishment, and they either sell someone out below them who takes the fall, or the issue just goes away. I guess it is easy to make crazy laws, if you know you don't have to abide by them.

Let us not forget once again that the government is *by the people, for the people.* During a campaign, so many politicians will promise one thing after another. But most of the time, they go right back to their own agendas as soon as they are elected, oftentimes betraying the very people who voted for them in the first place. For example, remember all the people who worked in the coal business, who were coerced into voting for Obama based on his campaign promises? Shortly after their votes were cast, he announced that he wanted to "clean up the coal industry," and many jobs in the industry were lost. All those in the coal business who voted for him must've felt betrayed, just like all the oil workers who lost their jobs due to Obama's offshore drilling moratorium.

My point is that people are elected based largely on what they say in their speeches prior to their elections. As much as President Obama said he supported the Second Amendment, you can see now he clearly does not. Once they are in office, there are no rules or laws to hold them to their campaign promises. The American people should be granted some power to hold the dishonest people on Capitol Hill accountable for their promises. You have probably heard the phrase "talk is cheap." I say this to all the elected officials: stick to your guns, no matter what; that's why you were elected in the first place.

For all you people out there who think there is a problem with America, while the everyday people own some responsibility for that, many of the problems of today's society are derived from crooked and poor leadership decisions on Capitol Hill and in the country's major financial institutions. For all you politicians, next time you bring an issue to the table, stop to think about if it is really important or if you are just making proposals to get your name in the history books. While you may hold all the cards now, think of the day when you won't. Would you want your government to go back on its word?

EIGHT

Military, Bureaucracy, and Their Deficiencies

The military, with its bureaucratic methodology, has become less efficient than it was intended to be. For instance, today, by rule of the law, if I have a question or a complaint, I'm not allowed to go straight to the top with it. Even if my concern is something that only affects the top, I am supposed to go to a guy who goes to a guy, who either gives some just-because answer or eventually goes to the top. And the response comes down the same way, which can be misinterpreted at any level. There are certain things for which this system works very well, but for the most part, it sucks to be a guy doing the job and having no impact on how it's done, especially when it's a job or a decision that may affect whether you live or die.

It seems that people in the military can't exercise the very rights they defend. Once again, you would not believe the grief I have gotten while trying to publish this book, and I'm sure I will endure much more for publishing it, even though it is my constitutional right. There is so much red tape with the military and they're not allowing me to publicly state my opinion or even certain facts because the party in question is messed up. They know it, and they can't handle being called on it. Is that not infringing on my freedom of speech that was granted to me for that very reason, so I could, in fact, speak out against the government without punishment? Seeing how I sacrificed nearly eighteen months of my life in Iraq for this country, I think I have earned that right.

ARE WE ROBOTS?

Having worked with other branches of the military over the years, I have realized that half the time most guys don't even know what they are doing or why they are doing it, like robots. Let's take, for example, the gate and outer wall guards of the base on my last deployment to Iraq. At the outer gate there were marines who were not even allowed to keep their weapons loaded; they maintained what is called "condition three." They also were not allowed to engage anyone or anything outside of twenty-five yards, no matter their activity. That is half the length of most swimming pools.

When asked about a structure less than three hundred yards away from the gate, a marine, who had personally guarded that duty station twelve hours a day for the last two months, had no idea what the structure was. To me, that was amazing. There's something you look at every day for sixty days, a structure from which a kill shot could easily be delivered, and you never thought to ask what it was. Wow! But I don't see that as entirely his fault. Most military, outside of spec war, is almost robotic. One kid was told to guard the gate. He was also taught to obey orders and not to ask questions. Does anyone see the problem with that? Those kids become reliant on a flawed system that doesn't allow the soldier to use his best weapon: his brain. Even in spec war, that weapon is being more and more subdued. People up top want to be listened to and obeyed unequivocally, even if they are not in the situation (and therefore can't know that it may warrant a different decision).

In 2007, my team had come under heavy enemy fire and was utilizing air strikes to cover our movement out of the area. Our commander, sitting in the nice, safe, barricaded mission control room, called a cease-fire for what was essentially our only cover at the time. I would have thought our ranking commander would understand that people in the field knew what was warranted in a situation such as that. Don't you think soldiers would be able to do a better job if they were not micromanaged, allowed to think independently and outside the box, but still followed orders? That's exactly how a good SEAL platoon works. People would also be able to do a better job if they knew more about the big picture. They could make better, more educated decisions based on more information, if they weren't treated as robots or idiots.

A classic example of this micromanaging was imposed on us in Iraq in the summer of 2009. A new rule was put in place by our commander that if, for whatever reason, a ground unit needed the use of Close Air Support (CAS) to neutralize enemies or threats, it was not at the discretion of the ground force commander, but the commanding officer of the unit or team back in the bunker.

Here's the problem with that strategy: if we, as a ground force, are being engaged, it adds another lengthy step to the suppression of that enemy fire. Instead of communicating directly to the aircraft and requesting the use of air-to-ground ordinance, I now had to communicate back to headquarters, have someone locate our *all-knowing* commanding officer (who is sitting safely on a guarded coalition base, not in a gun fight), brief him on the current situation, and receive his approval to save my team and me.

Tell me that is not a bureaucratic load of rubbish. Imagine if a teammate was fatally wounded during that request process; how do you explain to his wife, mother, or kids that he might have been alive had their government cared more about its warriors than its political progress or procedural formalities? Unfortunately, many of these types of regulations are imposed every day on US forces that are deployed in the interest of politics.

POLITICAL PROGRESS OR TACTICAL SUCCESS?

In my case, on my deployment in 2009, the war was winding down, and forces were moving out. I mentally prepared myself for that deployment and

> We were stuck wasting millions of taxpayer dollars to essentially be separated from our families for seven plus months.

for the fact that we were not going to be very busy operationally. The only problem was that there was more insurgent activity than there had been in a long time, yet we still were not able to operate. Our chain of command was so messed up that we were stuck wasting millions of taxpayer dollars to essentially be separated from our families for seven plus months.

While our local detachment would submit actionable intelligence, meeting all the criteria given to us, the people above them would always find some reason for us not to go and get these guys. Our chain of command even told us that one of our government agencies that deals solely with intelligence in the area wasn't a viable source, and they would not approve our mission, because we didn't generate our own intel. Who cares where the intel comes from, especially if it is coming from a government agency with the word *intelligence* in its title? Every reason they gave us was obviously a scheme to keep us from doing our jobs to avoid a political incident on their watch.

My suspicions were that there were politics involved, and it would look bad on someone's record high in the chain of command if "those SEALs" went out and, God forbid, killed some "innocent civilians with guns." My suspicions were confirmed when the team who relieved us at that outstation took one look at our objectives and immediately started auctioning those targets under the fresh leadership. The quote that made its way down the chain of command to me over the course of our deployment was, "We don't want to sacrifice political progress for tactical success." Well then, what are we doing here, General? Send us home and deploy a bunch of diplomats, if that's your mentality.

I know right now you are thinking, *Why would that be going on?* I asked myself that question the entire time I was there. The reason is still unknown to my lieutenant at the time or me. A common belief among the men was that our commanding officer was more interested in getting an award for completing a deployment as the commanding officer without an "incident" than he was about getting out there and getting bad guys, a classic example of commanders caring more about the next rank than the cause. I believe there are many reasons for it, but one reason that stands out is that most of the current commanders joined the military when there was no war and consequently have not seen much combat, if any. Therefore it is difficult for them to comprehend the logistics of war and the effectiveness of the boot on the ground.

The System

A big problem with the chain of command in the military is that, for the most part, whoever is in charge usually tries to micromanage everything, especially the people who hold roles that senior men once held. They always seem to think they did it better when it was their job. I have found that if they can't be a part of something and manage it directly, they don't want it to happen. There is little professional trust, even in the spec war community. I, for one, have lost so much faith in "the system." Very few people in power seem to care about anything but themselves, their careers, and making the next rank. Ironically, that's why they made rank in the first place.

The situation we were in on my last deployment was a classic example of system failure. We were not allowed to action targets (go on missions), so those targets stayed active and killed coalition forces or local Iraqis. Then our commanders would ask us why we were not targeting those people, and we would target them again. From that point, it went one of two ways. The first way was they would just not approve the target and give us some false line about how there was not enough intelligence, when there clearly was, it was too dangerous (war is inherently dangerous), or some other trash. The second way was that they just never answered us and tried to ignore it until the opportunity passed again, which would start the cycle over.

Eventually, when enough time had passed, we would, in the interest of making tactical progress, pass the target off to a unit that could get approved for the operation, and they would go hit the target. Once the other force hit the target with success, our chain of command would ask us why we gave the target away. Our detachment commander, who was one of the best leaders and people I have ever met, would usually send our head shed a message back, saying, "We tried to, but you guys would not approve it." There would be some sort of big meeting in which everyone was told things were going to change, but they never did. The frustration was overwhelming.

It's one thing if we were in Iraq and there was nothing to do, no bad guys to get, and no Americans getting killed, but that was not the case. Americans were being killed, and there were bad guys to get. The higher-ups didn't seem to care about that; they cared more about politics than they did about taking the right or necessary action. Our enemies knew that, and they knew we were pulling out of the country, so they ramped up the attacks, because they knew no one would stop them. Now tell me how it makes any sense to bring a multimillion-dollar fighting force all the way to Iraq just to sit on our bunks when there was good work for the cause to be done. So much for justice in the eyes of the taxpayers.

I may not have the whole story, but I believe it is your individual commander's duty to keep you informed of the big picture, as well as the little things. Fortunately, my detachment commander did a great job doing that, and everyone there at least had some information and didn't always have to sit around wondering about the next day. Information is not only crucial to the decision-making process, but it's also a huge help with morale. During an operation, the commanding officer back at base wants to know what the men are doing on the operation, and the men out on the ops want to know what the commander is doing that affects their operations. The lack of information given to most conventional forces hurts them more than withholding it helps.

DRINKING THE KOOL-AID

Sometimes you have to wonder at what point a guy goes from being one of the boys to being a total idiot in charge. We call it "drinking the Kool-Aid." I have had a few bosses that are great guys and not jerks, but they still command everyone's complete respect. Any boss that gives you the "I am not your friend, I'm your boss" speech is *demanding* respect because he knows he hasn't *earned* it. A good boss doesn't have to tell his men that. Under the command of such a boss, the men know when to answer him as such and when to be his friend, without anything ever being said.

Unfortunately, there are many officers, chiefs, and sergeants out there who may have been rational and approachable at one point, but who, as soon as they were given a little bit of power, quit making decisions based on the best interest of the mission and began making them based on the impact they would have on their careers. When that happens, you have ranking members of the command who start putting more effort into the appearance of their units via haircuts and squared-away uniforms than the actual mission. As an old quote says, "An inspection-ready unit has never been combat-ready, and a combat-ready unit has never been inspection-ready."

Those people let their egos get in the way, and they are usually the ones with no experience or chips on their shoulders because they were failures at their jobs when they were at lower ranks. They saw how their superiors came down on them because they sucked. Now they hold all the cards, and they think that is how you treat everyone, even if they are rock-star performers. I have had firsthand experience with people like that.

For example, one of the guys I worked for—the same kind of guy who gets fired from every job he's given yet still gets promoted—gave what I'm sure he believed was a rousing, inspirational, and thought-provoking speech regarding the changes he was making to our group. The premise of the speech was communication problems and the issues we were having passing information from the top of the chain to the bottom.

> How can you expect someone in a leadership position to execute directives as complex as winning a war when he conceptually believes he is flattening something by making it thicker?

To remedy the problem, we were going to *flatten* the organization. *Great idea,* I thought, *perhaps you are not utterly worthless.* No sooner had I thought that than he continued speaking, and I made a mental note to never second-guess my initial assessment. He said we were going to *flatten* the organization by *adding two extra layers* of management. What? Someone, somewhere had told this guy that he needed to flatten the organization, so he decided to do it. Unfortunately, there was clearly a major breakdown in his brain that caused him to do just the opposite. If you run this example to its end, you have some insight into why we are losing the Global War on Terror (GWOT). How can you expect someone in a leadership position to execute directives as complex as winning a war when he conceptually believes he is *flattening* something by making it *thicker?*

A RANK ISSUE

Those people are perfect examples of how you don't necessarily have to be good at your job to rise through the ranks in the military. You just have to do the following:

- put in your time

- be in the right place at the right time

- kiss up to the right people

- make sure that when you do work, everyone knows you did it, and emphasize how much you did

Follow these steps, and you will make rank faster than a humble, soft-spoken stud, who looks out for his boys. Those guys will eventually either get out and move on with their lives or stay in long enough to make the rank, long after the jerks are gone.

Let me run you through a brief but very common scenario of how many jerks make rank.

Me: "We have to fire this guy, he's incompetent, a horrible platoon lead petty officer (LPO), and he's going to get one of us killed."

Superior: "We can't fire him; how will it affect his career?"

Me: "I'm hoping it will end his career; he's clearly in the wrong line of work. That's why we fire people. We are better off without him; he is a liability."

Superior: "Let's just make a job for him that allows him to save face but ensures he has no responsibilities—how about Troop LPO?" (Troop LPO is a nonexistent position perceived to be higher than platoon LPO.)

Me: "But the problem with just creating a job with no responsibilities is that he's still eligible for promotion. That's why he has to be fired and kicked out of the community."

Superior: "You don't know what you're talking about; he'll stay out of the way in his new position."

Fast forward a week . . .

Superior to whole platoon: "Petty Officer Jerk has been promoted to the position of Troop LPO. "

Semi-observant guy knows Petty Officer Jerk is an idiot: "Why would they promote Petty Officer Jerk? He's an idiot, and what is a Troop LPO anyway?"

What happens: Petty Officer Jerk reports directly to, more often than not, stupid and unorganized head shed, befriending him prior to his promotion board.

Fast forward six months . . .

Promotion Board: "Look at this, Petty Officer Jerk was so good at his job that they promoted him to Troop LPO. This guy must be great."

Outnumbered Semi-observant Promotion Board member: "There's no such position; they probably made up the title to get rid of him."

Promotion Board: "That's not possible. He's obviously so good they created a new job for him."

Petty Officer Jerk's Immediate Superior to Board: "He has worked directly under me, and I say he's good to go, because I like him."

Two weeks later . . .

Superior to Platoon: I'm pleased to announce that Petty Officer Jerk has been promoted to Chief.

Me: (Stunned silence.)

Here is what confuses me most, though. All the sled dogs (the hardworking guys who actually carry out the orders) see right through the idiots and distance themselves from their antics, associating with them only as necessary for work. Yet, when good higher-ups come in—and I know every one of them was a workhorse at some time and has been through the ranks—they don't recognize their peers that suck. Maybe it's that the kiss-ups are just that good at it. Personally, I would rather be someone the guys trust and respect than make rank. Saying all that, there are some respectable high-rankers who can balance doing the right and honorable thing while playing politics. Those people are known as "solid dudes" or "rock stars," and are respected up and down the chain of command. They are also exponentially more efficient. The problem now, though, is that most of the "rock stars" are getting out, leaving the upper echelon as predominantly incompetent management.

STOP LOSS

To somewhat divert total collapse and avoid diminished numbers, the military instituted a program called "stop loss." There was even a fairly decent movie made about it called *Stop Loss*. Today our military is a volunteer program. For those of you who haven't served, the military treats their employees, who are willing to die for the country, like second-rate citizens. Even being a part of Naval Special Warfare, the highest funded and most relaxed community in the military, I still have shortfalls and deficiencies, and often lack the desired tools to complete the job. Many times we are told to "make do" with what we have. I can only imagine how a private in the army must be treated.

> The military treats their employees, who are willing to die for the country, like second-rate citizens.

The stop loss program is most common to the army. Many soldiers come home from as many as sixteen months of deployment and try to get out of the military, and the army says no. Hold on a second. These brave citizens signed a contract to serve their country, held up their end, and now they want to get out for whatever reason they may have. But the country that they just left everything behind and went to war for says, "Nope, forget your plans. We want more from you." I think this is completely wrong, and it's why we have people killing themselves and fellow soldiers overseas. For example, in Baghdad in May 2009, a soldier opened fire on his colleagues while in a support center on base. I haven't found any evidence to say he was stop lossed, but he had been deployed three times for an unnecessarily long amount of time. Are these selfless men and women entitled to any rights?

SYSTEM DEFICIENCIES

While I have touched on most of the finer issues with bureaucracy, I would like to go into some of the broader points that illustrate deficiencies of this system. Less than half the people in these jobs among unions, the military, or other government-regulated systems take pride in their work. They know that they only have to work hard enough to not get fired. In the case of the military, they know they must always have a third party outside the chain of command on whom to blame deficiencies.

I have more examples of this than I can count, but one that stands out was regarding my paycheck. Upon checking into a new command, my pay was disrupted, and I was being shorted about six hundred dollars per pay period, which equaled $1,200 a month. I reported it and was told that it would be fixed immediately and that I would see the back pay in my next paycheck. When my next paycheck came, I was not surprised to see that it had not been fixed. I again brought it to the attention of my command representative. His response was immediately defensive, saying he'd filed the paperwork weeks ago and blamed another department for the mistake.

Since I was approaching my third consecutive incorrect paycheck, I called the department he'd blamed, and they told me there had been no paperwork filed on my pay deficiency—now nearing $1,800—and that they would call me as soon as the issue was resolved. Being the confrontational person that I am, I brought this information back to the command representative. His response was, "Well, I have been so busy I haven't had time to get around to it." This liar had just finished telling me that he'd filed that paperwork weeks ago, and now he was telling a different story. That would get you fired in a real job. So, remember the faith I have in the chain of command?

I next told my boss, who called the command rep's boss, who talked to him. His boss then called my boss back and told him the same false story about the failure of the other department. That liar had told his boss the same lie he had originally told me, and nothing was accomplished. There was another month of confrontation with similar lack of resolution, until finally I was able to request a meeting with his boss, him, my boss, and me. I laid out the situation with all of the documentation I had collected on the deficiencies, now totaling nearly $3,000. A five-minute call was made on the spot, the problem was fixed, and my next paycheck was a few thousand dollars fatter.

Once the problem had been resolved, I wanted to take disciplinary action against the command representative to illustrate the seriousness of his action. I was told by both his boss and mine, "Let it go, Carl; you got your money." The point was that, if you just let things like this go unaddressed, then they will surely happen again. I was told to back off and it would be dealt with, which it never was. Another chain-of-command failure.

Two months later, a similar situation happened to another member of the command, only he didn't have the money in pocket to cover the deficiency. He was late on a mortgage payment and paid late fees as a result of it. Needless to say, the same idiot is still assigned to these matters in the navy today, with no disciplinary action taken over a year later. Even more distressing, upon his changing commands, during his closeout evaluation and farewell, he received a medal of recognition for his service to the command. I just shrug my shoulders and shake my head in dismay.

The issue was not that he didn't have the time or didn't know how to do it; it's just that there was no motivation to get it done, because in the military it's nearly impossible to fire people. In contrast, imagine yourself working for a *Fortune 500* company and not getting paid properly over a three-month period. Would you go to human resources, stop coming to work, or file a lawsuit? The point is, things like this are not tolerated outside the military or other bureaucratic federal agencies. Really, is it too much to ask to take pride in a job that reflects on your own image?

The DMV

I know nearly every American has been to the Department of Motor Vehicles (DMV) and will know what I mean when I say that I consider every government-run establishment a DMV. The DMV is a model of why the government should not have any control over our personal lives. Walking in there is like stepping into a wormhole.

There are always a thousand people there, all the lines are mislabeled, and there are fifty people standing behind the counter doing nothing while one employee helps people. The person working that window usually has no idea what he is doing and has to ask the fifty other idle people about everything you need, because the employees rarely seem to have an education over a GED. On top of that, there has inevitably been some new law imposed recently that says you need to have one more piece of paper, which you obviously don't have.

Whenever I need to go to the DMV for anything, I always consider the full day as a complete write-off. Cases like this are why people think the government is so inefficient. I'm sure if it were easier to fire people holding government positions, or make them have any accountability at all, there would be remarkable improvement. I'm not holding my breath, though. Could you imagine if Congressman Charles Rangel had worked for NASDAQ and was implicated on such charges? He would have been canned instantly.

Though I do hate the way our military is run, I would not take back a day of my time served. There are tons of instances that have nearly given me an aneurism, but every part about it was a learning experience. I was given the opportunity to serve with some of the best men this country has to offer. The experiences I have endured have shaped my life and character. This goes to show that life is what you make of it.

NINE

Idealism vs. Realism

Everyone is either a realist or an idealist; there really isn't a middle ground. The idealist is someone who usually has good intentions with their ideas and plans, but their plan usually requires living in a perfect world or some other farfetched version of reality. It's a world without greed or evil, a place where everything works out and everyone is willing to give a little and only take a little. While I do believe that mankind is inherently good, people have been tainted by the greed of society and have become selfish, swayed by materialistic values.

I know that not everyone will always agree, and not everyone wants the same things. That is why we live in a real world and not an ideal world. These methods of thinking, such as negotiating with terrorists or regimes like Iran and Al-Qaeda, are just one of the many weaknesses of the idealistic philosophy. There are too many people on the left who think everyone out there is willing to negotiate. Did we negotiate with England when they wanted to over tax us? And why would North Korea let us micromanage or even ban their nuclear program? With this ideology, we open ourselves up to failure by simply believing that things will inherently get better.

Another problem with idealism is that there are so many people out there with so many interpretations of what constitutes an ideal world. In order for this philosophy to hold any practicality in execution, there would have to be a definitive model of what an ideal world is. Mine is very different from Joe Biden's, for example. If the idealist state existed, it would be forever disappointing someone. That's just the reality of the situation (realism).

> Obviously 9/11 wasn't enough proof, so it falls on us now to protect America from falling apart.

Realists are people who are generally more down-to-earth and have backup plans, because they know that at any point life could change, and they might have to endure the worst. "Hope for the best and plan for the worst" is my motto. This real-world thinking is what saves this country when the idealists run out of great ideas. The best analogy I can provide for this thinking is that the realists are the parents, and the idealists are the children with no knowledge of evil in the world. Well, realist, it's time to step up and teach the naïve people in the world how things really work. Obviously 9/11 wasn't enough proof, so it falls on us now to protect America from falling apart. Unfortunately, it is the responsibility of realists to look out for the weak as well. By choosing this lifestyle and mind-set, we have inherited much responsibility.

GETTING REAL

Another example is the debt-ceiling debate. Here we are as a country with nearing $15 trillion of debt, and the Democrats, with a small trail of Republicans, want to raise the debt ceiling. Once again, I may not be fully informed, but I see this as a catastrophic mistake. When does it stop? Many Republicans are willing to shut down the government in order to strike a cord of reality to stop spending. At some point, you cannot continue to borrow money. There comes a point when enough people will ask for their money back that it cannot be repaid, or the interest on the debt will become so unsustainable that our government will default. Again, that is reality.

I have a lot of friends I would identify as realists, who still think I'm overly prepared, but as long as it's not hurting anyone, why not be ready? Yes, I do have a trunk full of worst-case scenario gear, such as food, water, camping supplies, and a substantial amount of firepower. Foreign invasion, riots, aliens, zombies, and even Obama's health care—I'm ready for it all. Do I think it will ever happen? Probably not, but if it does, I'll be ready. And all you folks who told me I was crazy, I might have a little extra for you. Hope for the best, plan for the worst.

My thinking behind this is that you can never be too prepared. Having seen intense combat up close and very personal while fighting for my own life, I know how bad things can get very quickly. If you prepare not only materially, but also mentally, in the unlikely event that a situation of that magnitude ever does present itself, you are ten steps ahead of everyone else. That allows people like me to help those who are inevitably unprepared, not because of any law, but because of the goodwill in my heart.

While growing up, I always thought my parents seemed to have a solution to any problems my friends or I had. Being kids, we took their advice as gospel, because it was some sort of direction. Now I have found that kids who ask questions expect answers, and sometimes almost any answer will do. I believe this is a vital realist tactic. A well-executed bad plan is better than a badly executed great plan, meaning that sometimes you have to just make a decision and act on it.

I see more and more unrealistic idealists on Capitol Hill, talking about things for what seems like forever without offering any real solutions, as President Obama did during the debt debates, and then the realist comes in and acts on it. While President Obama has made some very good speeches, that's really all he's done; there has been very little action from the administration to date, outside the sodomy that is the disastrous health care bill. Vice President Biden said the second one hundred days would bring much more action, but I never saw it. I'm really not expecting much, considering there's rarely any sense in Vice President's Biden's statements.

SOCIALISM IN AMERICA

While back on the topic of the Obama administration's faults, I want to talk more about the near-socialist state we are coming closer to every day. With General Motors (GM), which was the first major company that temporarily fell into federal power, we are getting closer and closer to the Marxist dream. The proposals of taxing the rich and giving handouts to the lazy are not the answer. Giving people a means and motivation to succeed is. Once again, that is America's foundation. The idealistic mentality is blinding people into thinking that everything will always turn out fine, and the government will solve everything. The rest of the world is rioting and crumbling because of this system.

Look at Egypt, where they were rioting in the streets because they didn't want the current governmental control. London was in shambles over the proposed tuition increase, most of Europe's market is shaky at best, Greece is nearly financially deceased, and other places around the world are rising up against socialist, dictatorship-style government "intervention," or as I call it, control, yet America is still trying to go the same route. As Glenn Beck observed, "We are becoming more and more like the governments that the rest of the world is trying to get away from."

LBJ's affirmative action plan, while a noble idea, was an idealistic plan that often allows less-qualified people to take a job from the better-qualified people. That contradicts the very equal-opportunity mantra by which affirmative action's supporters live. As I mentioned earlier, a lot of people who worked hard to gain a professional advantage are being discriminated against because of their race or ethnicity.

Communism is an idealist strategy that has failed in every government application since its début, leaving catastrophic fallout that lasts for years. Things like equal health care, Medicare, and standardized wages and benefits have crushed empires such as the Soviet Union. Cuba is still a Communist state, and in the midst of trying to supply everyone with everything, it has collapsed and become a model of poverty, supplying no one with anything. On paper, Communism seems like a great idea that should work, but applied to a real-world model, it is destined for failure, as has been proven repeatedly throughout history.

> Now we have a president who receives support and funding from people and organizations that openly support Communism.

Being a realist, I know that we can't just give, give, and give to the people without the people giving back. It is up to you and no one else to provide for your family and you. Lest we forget, during the Cold War, people were deported, imprisoned, and punished for even uttering thoughts of Communism here in America. Now we have a president who receives support and funding from people and organizations that openly support Communism. Thank God for a president like Reagan, who was one of the few politicians willing to do anything to put a stop to this kind of thinking. We need someone like that to recover from this regime's antics. If Reagan were alive today, he would have a few choice words about the way things are going. He certainly would not approve of being featured on the cover of *Time* magazine with Obama under the similarities of "optimism."

WESTERN DEMOCRACY

Even more idealistic than a functional Communist state is the attempt at imposing Western democracy in Iraq. The problem with this idea is that, no matter how much sense our form of government makes to us, Iraq and countries currently in the same ideology as Iraq do not have the same mentality as Americans. Many things are engrained in their culture that prevent them from having any sort of organized or civil government or society. Violence is usually the only language these people speak in terms of leadership. If you have a bigger gun, then you are in charge. Negotiations are not a preliminary step and are usually out of the question. Look at how Saddam Hussein did it, and America helped put him in power. In the early eighties, the Reagan administration helped place Saddam into power in an effort to maintain our access to the oil fields and prevent Iran from seizing control of the region's resources. As great a president as Reagan was, that was a totally idealistic power play. We knew Saddam was a murderous dictator, and we thought we could reason with him.

Iraq is nowhere nearly sophisticated enough to adhere to the complexities of Western democracy. Most people in Iraq don't even care about political policy. The other big problem democracy faces in the Middle East is that democracy is a form of government that, for the most part, at least attempts to hold people accountable for their actions. Once again, from firsthand experience, I can tell you that Iraq is a culture in which there is little competition or accountability for anything.

There is a term in most of the Muslim world, *insha Allah*. It means "God willing" or "God willed it." I have personally witnessed someone being asked what one plus one is and replying, "Two *insha Allah*." It's a mathematical equation, you moron—two is the answer whether God or anyone else wills it or not. If people make mistakes or do something wrong, they throw this phrase out in order to pass blame. If you honestly think this type of lifestyle will support anything higher than chaos and failure, I suggest you get a CAT scan. Imagine this health care bill destroying America and Obama saying, *"Insha Allah"* as the country goes down the drain. I'm sure he would end up blaming it on Bush instead.

America has pumped billions of dollars into a war that holds no benefit for even the people of the country for whom we say we are fighting. These people have been killing each other over religion and tribal disputes for thousands of years; they teach their children to kill the *infidel* (non-Muslim). I can't imagine that they will suddenly see that the strategies and ideas of their sworn enemy are right and spontaneously change their primitive and destructive lifestyle. Sorry, but you can't fight this or any war with an idealistic method. If you want to win at this or any war, you will have to offend and, at times, kill people. A lot of them.

A realistic approach to this country would be to say, "Guess what, Iraq. You are harboring terrorists, and we are going to get them. You are either part of the solution or part of the problem." I know so many countries in the world hate America for its aggression and straightforwardness. But the radical Muslims who attacked us on 9/11, some of whom were trained and harbored in Iraq or Afghanistan, came into our country, killed our citizens, and destroyed our towers. That is an act of war, and the whole Middle East is lucky America didn't declare war on the region because they knowingly harbored these outlaws. We should have instantly declared war on Pakistan as soon as we learned that Osama Bin Laden's compound was less than a decent four-iron shot from the nearest Pakistani military outpost. Many of these countries don't give a rip about America, even though we give them billions of dollars.

> The spineless, idealistic views of modern government are tearing us apart while claiming they are supposed to bring us together.

Those are the *real* facts of the situation. Why are we destroying our own credibility and unity just so Iraq, Afghanistan, or any other country we may be fighting a war in can call the shots on how we resolve a situation that started by an act of war against America? The spineless, idealistic views of modern government are tearing us apart while claiming they are supposed to bring us together. President Obama campaigned on unity and change for the better. His idealistic views and policies have divided our nation more than ever before.

America, it's time to get real!

TEN

The Obamanation and His Administration

I want to start by talking about President Obama and the fiasco called an election. The *Association of Community Organizations for Reform Now* (ACORN) registered countless voters in the months leading up to the presidential election. Some of those voters were later found to be deceased at the time they supposedly cast their votes. Stuff like that would be comical if it weren't true, but our nation's future is being determined by some of the voters and organizations that tried ridiculous antics like that.

If it were up to me, you would have to prove you are worthy in order to be able to vote. If you have done nothing but take your whole life, then you probably should not be able to vote. With the number of voters receiving government aid rising to over 50 percent, the candidate who promises the most handouts will probably control future elections (Democrats). Years ago, only the upper class landowners were allowed to vote; that was a blanket screening system to keep ignorant and uneducated people from voting so individual votes couldn't be bribed with something as simple as a pack of cigarettes (as ACORN did).

THE Q & A JOKE

Fox News aired a clip of one of their reporters going around the streets of New York City, asking people for whom they were voting. If they answered Obama, they were subjected to a few other questions that were of totally voluntary participation.

One of those questions was, "What do you think about Obama's running mate, Sarah Palin?"

The response from one black person was, "I think it's great! They are really going to turn this country around."

And these people are allowed to vote? When informed that Palin was, in fact, McCain's running mate, they were obviously embarrassed and had nothing else to say, but I bet they still voted.

A number of people were asked questions, such as, "What do you think about Obama's health care proposal—the use of tax credits and a more competitive insurance marketplace?" (McCain's proposal)

When I saw that the response was, "Oh, I think it's great," I was in shocked disbelief, especially considering that Obama's socialist-style version of health care was one of the most widely publicized topics of the election. If you're putting your name on a ballot, you might want to know a thing or two about the person who could very well determine the course of the next four years of your life.

If you don't know something, it's okay to say so, but since I was for McCain, I encouraged idiots like the above to continue looking like idiots on national television. I know what you Democrats are thinking right now: *There are plenty of times Republicans look like idiots.* Yes, that's true, but if you had asked me on the street what I thought of McCain's education reform plan, I would have said, "Sorry, I'm not really sure what his plan is." I would not just blindly support a statement some reporter told me on the street.

Congratulations, President Obama, the victory is truly yours. As for us outnumbered, educated people, better luck in 2012. But after the message people sent in 2010, starting with the election of Scott Brown as the first Republican senator from Massachusetts in over thirty years, and continuing with Republicans gaining over sixty seats in the House of Representatives— putting Pelosi in the backseat—and six seats in the United States Senate, I feel pretty good about the American people waking up.

I feel pretty good about the American people waking up.

For my own amusement one day, I asked a question to someone standing next to me in line at Quiznos. Two black people were discussing how much they approved of Obama. Okay, fine, that's your opinion, but I was curious. So, pretending I was also for Obama, I said, "Yeah, I really hope he wins, too, but what do you think about his plans for guns? Don't you think encouraging every American to buy a gun could get a little dangerous?" knowing full well that he had tried his hardest to ban guns in Illinois.

"No, that's a great idea. It'll help the streets." *Okay, idiot,* I thought, *aside from the fact that your pants are six inches below your rear end (and Obama did say "brothers gotta pull their pants up"), you should be voting for McCain and Palin, if you agree with that.* With three people still ahead of me in line, I continued to mess with them.

"What do you like best about his tax reform?"

I could see the wheels turning when they said, "Well, I just really like what he stands for. He's really looking out for the people." Good cop-out, dingbat.

Let's be honest. Obama won first and foremost because he was black. The unprecedented number of black voters that turned out for that election is an undeniable statistic; Obama even won Virginia. The second thing that won people over is that he was not Bush. Bush had been smeared so badly by the mainstream media over his last term that people wanted the opposite of him, no matter who the candidate was. I would like to hand the Darwin award to the majority of the country that voted for someone who never served in the military, did cocaine openly, was openly known to be one of the most liberal senators ever, and who we weren't even sure was born in America.

OBAMA'S UPSIDE-DOWN STRATEGY

The Obama administration turned this country upside down in less than half a term. Giving him the benefit of the doubt, I think he always pushed for what he thought was best for the country; it's just that his views of what is best are as radical and backward as it gets. Here are some of the despicable actions he has taken so far:

- One of the first things he did when he took office was to apologize to the whole world for how America imposes itself on everyone. He even bowed to the king of Saudi Arabia and the emperor of Japan, which is an act of submission.

- He decided to prosecute the men who did work on GITMO detainees that saved American lives.

- He put terrorists up for regular criminal trials, with Constitutional rights, in America.

- He tried to tax and impose the government's influence on the hard workers of American small businesses after promising no new taxes during his campaign.

- He promised on more than one occasion to be transparent and publicly televise health care negotiations on C-SPAN, and then held them behind closed doors.

- He spent trillions of dollars on bailouts and "special programs" to create jobs that seemed to never come.

- He sent hundreds of millions of dollars that we didn't have in aid to foreign countries.

- He visited Chicago instead of Arlington National Cemetery on Memorial Day.

- Worst of all, he imposed a national health care bill on the country that nearly 70 percent of Americans didn't want.

- In addition to all that, during two wars and a recession, he managed to squeeze in four times as many rounds of golf in eighteen months as Bush did in eight years, not to mention the six vacations he took.

Really! I ask again, how could anyone be happy with the decision to elect someone so detached from the responsibilities of the leader of the most powerful country in the world? And if you are, give me one good reason why.

A FRIGHTENING COMPARISON

I want to reference an article that was sent to me by a close family friend. The author of this article lives in South Dakota and is very active in attempting to maintain our freedom. Her name is Kitty Werthmann, and the article is "America Truly is the Greatest Country in the World. Don't Let Freedom Slip Away." The article is entirely based on fact and the firsthand experience of a young girl living in Austria. It takes place prior to and during World War II.

Contrary to popular belief, Adolph Hitler did not take Austria by force; he was, in fact, elected by an overwhelming majority under the promise of a nearly perfect society. Today much of this is lost in the liberal historic teachings of public school, but it is true. People were so upset with over 30 percent unemployment and nearly the same inflation rate that they were open to any "change." The situation was far worse than ours here today in America, but it nevertheless mirrored some of the same problems we face now. Jobs were being lost, businesses were going under, and people could barely afford food. Werthmann's mother did what she could to help by making as much food as they could afford to share with people in need.

In a wide-eyed hypnosis, Austria looked to Germany for support after hearing of their nearly perfect society through propaganda and word of mouth. Soon after the peaceful takeover by the German government, there were an abundance of government jobs through public works projects. Sound familiar yet?

As Werthmann wrote, "The day we elected Hitler (March 13, 1938), I walked into my schoolroom to find the crucifix replaced by Hitler's picture hanging next to a Nazi flag." After Hitler was elected, the previously Catholic public schools changed, and religion was disbanded. Crosses were replaced with the Nazi flag and other icons from his regime. Sound like today's liberal screams of separation of church and state? Students were suddenly required to attend government programs; if they did not, their families would be fined or even jailed. Hmm, fined for not participating in a government program—sounds a lot like Obama's health care plan. See where I am going with this?

Werthmann's mother wisely pulled Kitty from the school and placed her in a convent. Though it was tough, she pushed through. On her occasional returns home, she was amazed at the unstructured lifestyle of her former peers. Hitler had loosened standards on everything from morals to reproduction. Everyone still tracking on how the Democratic progressives have done similar things in regards to proposing lowering standards in schools and morals? Remember the instance of the Boulder, Colorado, high school assembly that went unpunished?

There was a push from the Nazi regime to incorporate women in everything, much as Obama pushed Supreme Court Judge Sotomayor into her current position over more qualified applicants, and how we are being forced to accept Muslim culture as a part of the American way.

This statement from Werthmann is a kicker too: "After Hitler, health care was socialized, . . . Doctors were salaried by the government. . . . the hospitals were full. If you needed elective surgery, you had to wait a year or two." All the money that had previously been poured into research was then redirected to fund socialized health care. The best doctors left or closed their doors because it was not worth it for them to continue their practice there."

Scared yet? If not, this next part should send you over the edge: "We had another agency designed to monitor business. . . . If the government owned the large businesses and not many small ones existed, it could be in control." Hello, GM, cap and trade, and federalizing financial institutions!

"Next came gun registration. . . . Hitler said that the real way to catch criminals . . . was by matching serial numbers on guns. Most citizens . . . dutifully marched to the police station to register their firearms." Once all the guns were registered, the government knew you had them. The authorities then told everyone to turn them in, and if you didn't, they would find you.

Then came freedom of speech. "Anyone who said something against the government was taken away." Have we not seen the Obama administration try to regulate what can and cannot be said over airwaves and what should be allowed on the Internet?

> Have we not seen the Obama administration try to regulate what can and cannot be said over airwaves and what should be allowed on the Internet?

Totalitarianism came gradually. Here is how Hitler did it, which is not unlike what is happening with the slow introduction of government programs here in America. "It took five years . . . to realize full dictatorship in Austria. Had it happened overnight, my countrymen would have fought to the last breath. Instead, we had creeping gradualism." Slowly but surely Hitler had taken the country over without force and, for the most part, with the support of the people. He had taken their youth by means of indoctrinating the schools, made them dependant on the government by way of their "shovel-ready jobs," and taken their guns, the only way to defend and rise up against an intrusion just like this. This is the "gradualism" that is coming out of our current administration—compare your government and its policies and direction to six years ago.

Werthmann closes with this simple but profound statement: "Don't let freedom slip away."

WAKE UP, AMERICA!

Does anything sound familiar in Kitty Werthmann's article? Wake up, America! Even after all these similarities, people still have arguments about how great Obama is and how he has done such great things for the country. Wake up! I am not saying Obama is going to slaughter millions of people, but he is a snake in the grass nevertheless. While I do believe his intentions are good in his eyes, he is setting this country on track for a piece of the ultimate global government. When he has been associated with people like radical liberal George Soros, who has nearly collapsed governments, and Van Jones, who has historically been detrimental to capitalism, why do people not see where we are headed? There is a reason why aspects of history, such as Werthmann details, are not taught in today's public schools. The progressive agenda does not want us to see it coming. The "powers that be" are trying to push us into a form of government that is not the true American way. We need to derail this trend and pull the carpet out from under these people.

Open your eyes and ask yourself why you like Obama so much. Really ask yourself and think about the answer. Because when I ask most people who support him to name one good thing he has done, I usually get the same old, "Well, he's getting the economy back on track," or "He's made so many new jobs," or "He is getting us out of the debt that Bush put us in," and a few more that are equally vague and foolish.

My initial response is always the same: *"What?"* or "Are you kidding me?" followed by my telling them how stupid they are, because I learn from history and think before I vote! They almost always challenge me until I break out my iPhone and show them rock-solid statistics on how Obama has spent us into massive debt, from federal websites, such as whitehouse.gov, contradicting their spacey "facts." Then this is my favorite part: they tell me those stats aren't right, are outdated or biased, despite their coming from a recently updated federal website, written by the current administration itself. I just write them off or ask my first question again. Come on, people, this is a crucial time in the history of this nation. Pull your heads out of the sand and get a grip on reality.

THE BLAME GAME

Obama has spent most of his press time blaming Bush for everything, including things for which he himself campaigned. He is doing it because he is distracting you from what is really going on. Isn't it funny that not one of the Democrats campaigned on the health care bill they passed during the 2010 mid-term elections? Health care is something that a great majority of Democrats supported, promised it would create jobs and fix the national deficit, and everything else shy of a perfect world, and not a single person campaigned on it. That is because they know it's wrong for us, and they only pushed it because they thought it would be good for their careers at the time. In fact, most of the Democrats' campaign ads were based on unconfirmed and unverifiable statistics. That's because Obama and his posse haven't done anything worth talking about. So, to redirect ownership of our nation's instability, they make up numbers and blame Bush.

Case in point: I got into an argument with a family member a little while ago over the national debt and recent absurd spending. He informed me that the current state of the economy was all due to Bush and how the war effort spent us into a massive deficit and that Obama has made things so much better. He proceeded to tell me, "It's a fact that Obama has made this country better in the short time he has been president (which at the time was eighteen months)." Now, mind you, this kid was twenty-one years old, didn't even vote, and had no factual basis for his claims, except other people's opinions. I showed him this annual deficit chart from whitehouse.gov. For the sake of simplicity, I have superimposed who ran the House and Senate and who was president, with their corresponding political party colors:

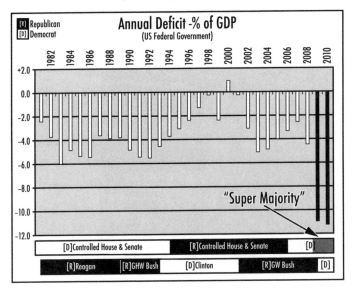

I proceeded to explain the principles behind the Bush defense budget of less than 5 percent of the GDP, which was lower than that of both Clinton and Obama. I told him briefly about the housing bubble; while not completely exonerating Bush, it was not entirely his fault. This chart and my other facts clearly squashed his opinions of how the Democrats have made things better. Along with losing his temper, he told me I was the idiot, and I didn't know what I was talking about. There is no reasoning with people like that.

A lot of these people are the ones who heavily criticized Bush for being too stupid to run the country for how he pronounced the word "nuclear," but when Obama said he had visited "fifty-seven states with a few more to go," they wrote it off as a teleprompter mistake, even though there was no teleprompter. Maybe I missed something, but I'm pretty sure there are only fifty states. Our president also took the opportunity to say there was "undeniable evidence of global warming," even though 2009–2010 had one of the coldest winters I have seen in a long time, and early 2011 showed record snowfall in some places. I would love to hear the logic on that one.

GLOBAL WARMING

I have heard the new theories buzzing around that say global warming is actually a misnomer for the planet having "extreme weather," but let's not forget what started the global warming craze. It was originally proposed as holes in the ozone near the North Pole supposedly caused by chlorofluorocarbons (CFCs) and carbon emissions. We were warned that the polar ice caps were melting because humans have done irreversible damage to the ozone, which is now letting in more of the sun's heat and radiation, hence the name "global warming."

Maybe I'm the moron, but as far as I understand it, *global warming* means the planet is in fact getting warmer, which makes sense based on the original evidence and claims, hence less snow and warmer temperatures. Maybe the president is spending too much time with Al Gore, the man who made a career out of global warming, warning the world that the seas would rise astronomically by 2010 due to polar icecaps melting. Not long after that statement, though, he bought a multi-million-dollar waterfront estate. The word *idiot* comes to mind.

How about when our commander in chief phonetically pronounced "corpsman" with a verbal "p" three times in the same speech, despite its being pronounced "coreman" with a silent "p"—I mean, really? Did you grow up under a rock? Everyone may not know how to pronounce that word, but our Commander-in-Chief should. Way to make Harvard proud. He repealed the "Don't ask; don't tell" policy, now allowing openly gay people to serve in the military. Our military has been successful and dominant so far with that policy in place, so why would you change it? It's asking for confrontation and instability. These are yet more examples of why someone should not be able to be the commander in chief without serving in the military.

STATE OF THE UNION

I want to cover Obama's first and second State of the Union speeches. Let's start by looking at how he entered the room both times. He came in like a rock star. This posture really makes me wonder if he is in the White House to do something for this country or to soak up the publicity. For the first speech, let's look at Tweedledee and Tweedledum, Biden and Pelosi. Those two idiots led ninety-three rounds of applause during his 2009 speech, some of which were standing ovations. During his second address, with four fewer Supreme Court justices in attendance, there were only eighty ovations, none of them led by newly elected speaker John Boehner. Seriously, nothing he said was so profound that anyone needed to interrupt with applause. Both speeches were over an hour long, with only about five minutes of worthwhile content.

Obama threw out a few low blows about the Bush administration during his first address, essentially blaming it for our current economic condition over a year later. During the second, he didn't pass as much blame, but he also did not once address the national rejection of his policies. He announced a spending freeze both times. For those of you who didn't catch the well-illustrated breakdown of it on *The Glenn Beck Show*, this would *freeze*, not cut, less than .01 percent, or less than a tenth of one percent of his current spending policy. Hey, Mr. President, you need to cut, not freeze, some of those big numbers that you have already blown. This was a great attempt at convincing the public that you are cutting your spending and that the Obama administration had no part in the current state of the economy.

> We have to vote him out of office in 2012, or I fear this recession will not end, and the country will suffer irreparable damage.

During his more recent address, he claimed the economy was growing as a result of the Bush tax cuts that *he* extended, even though when they were debating the bill, he said it would have a negative effect on the country. He wanted to "out-innovate, out-educate, and out-build." But how can we do that with all of Obama's proposed stipulations on industry in this country? It's much like the congressional bypass he performed by having the Environmental Protection Agency (EPA) declare CO_2 as a pollutant in order to tax companies more. He tried to instill faith in the government by stating, "The American people deserve to know." Where was that during your health care debates, which resulted in a bill you now state will cost America a quarter of a trillion dollars to repeal?

The second State of the Union address was about as hollow as the first. It was just more justification on spending as an "investment in our future" and all the work he has done that has benefited this country so much. He is a talker, a used-car salesman running the country with the aid of a teleprompter. We have to vote him out of office in 2012, or I fear this recession will not end, and the country will suffer irreparable damage.

REALITY CHECK

Now as much as I would like to blame the recession all on Obama, the following is what truly caused the recession. This article, entitled "Meltdown Simplified," is from the website removethemall.us and *Reality Check*, a book co-authored by Dennis Keegan and a close family friend, David West, who were happy to have it included in this book. They are extremely well informed and intelligent men, and I think they hit the nail right on the head. They wrote this:

It would be hard to overstate the importance to the future of our financial system, and thus our country, of a clear and broad understanding of what caused—and what did not cause—the recession of 2009–10. We cannot allow ignorance to reign.

Everyone agrees that the bursting of a real estate bubble caused the meltdown. What caused the bubble? Too many mortgages were chasing a fixed number of homes. Most people understand supply and demand, but for those who need a refresher—if you have ten Big Macs and twelve hungry buyers, the price could easily rise from the usual $3.50 to $6.00 before two buyers decide to go without.

What created more mortgages? Start with Fannie Mae and Freddie Mac, which were established by the government decades ago to help a small number of struggling households buy homes. "Fannie & Freddie" had become involved in over two-thirds of all new mortgages by the end of the housing bubble. They were accepting riskier mortgages from banks with increasingly lower documentation standards. Why? Being quasi-government organizations, everyone assumed that if things blew up, they would be bailed out. They were right. Who is to blame for this? Consider this headline from the *New York Times*, dated September 11, 2003: "The Bush administration today recommended the most significant regulatory overhaul in the housing finance industry since the savings and loan crisis a decade ago." This overhaul never happened. Democrats claimed it was a veiled attack on affordable housing and firmly asserted that all was fine at Fannie Mae.

Secondly, the Community Reinvestment Act—passed by Carter and expanded by Clinton—encouraged banks to make loans in low-income neighborhoods. Good intent, but encouraging banks to make riskier loans runs counter to encouraging discipline and prudence. How do overseers simultaneously sue banks for not making enough risky loans while also telling them they are taking on too much risk?

These two factors alone were not enough to create the housing bubble. Enter the big gorilla, the Federal Reserve Bank, or the "Fed." Keeping interest rates too low for too long in the mid 2000s pushed more and more money into credit markets. Much of this money made its way through the path of least resistance—as a result of the environment described above—to mortgages. Voilà, a housing bubble. Too much money and too many mortgages were chasing a fixed number of homes. Ten burgers, twelve buyers. The Fed is a government institution. Once again government intervention is at fault.

Real estate prices went up nearly 90 percent in five short years. Then when oil shock hit, and people actually couldn't afford the risky mortgages, defaults and reduced demand reversed the cycle. Crash.

Notice that the biggest causes of the crisis involved government intervention—Fannie, Freddie, CRA, and actions by the Fed. Well-intentioned legislation often has unintended negative consequences. This was not a failure of the free market. It was the opposite. It was a failure of government intervention.

Much has been made of the lack of Wall Street oversight. This is more complicated, but the bursting of the housing bubble can be thought of as a big tree that came crashing down on top of another tree—financial institutions—which then also crashed. Newfangled financial instruments (credit default swaps, derivatives, etc.), which were designed to hedge the risk, or help prop it up if the big tree ever started to fall, were themselves rotten. These safety nets were designed to catch a bank if it fell, but were not able to catch all the banks if they fell at once. Looking at just their own safety net and not the broader, "systemic" risk encouraged banks to take even greater risks, borrowing more than was prudent. One can blame one group or another for oversight failures here, but (a) the wisest sages—Greenspan, Bernanke, and the bankers who lost everything when it collapsed—did not see the risk, by their own admission, and (b) if the big tree hadn't fallen in the first place, the second tree wouldn't have been crushed. So, we must go back to what caused that big tree to collapse—back to the housing bubble and government intervention.

The other false culprit is "greed." Greed, or acting in one's self-interest, is a part of the human condition—no greater today than ten, fifty, or a thousand years ago. Blaming greed doesn't stand up to cause-and-effect scrutiny at the most rudimentary level. Is the claim that a small group of people somehow had the power to cause a basic human characteristic to surge among millions of people, making home values rise? No, something changed. See above.

Trying to fix problems caused by government intervention with more government intervention is unlikely to succeed. Bankers will not repeat the mistakes of the past, with or without oversight. Markets and experience do a great job of preventing this. But if the government again causes disruption through intervention, as it appears to be doing with "too big to fail" bailouts, excessively low Fed rates, and propping up mortgages that should fail, US citizens will probably pay—again.[2]

Bailouts. The bailout was another topic that was exaggerated and blown out of proportion in the State of the Union. Obama said that it saved over two million jobs—what is the source of those statistics? Unemployment rose to over 10 percent, and even though it was reportedly down in the government's eyes after his address, those numbers are flawed, because they don't account for the people who have stopped looking for jobs or haven't filed for unemployment, which brings the actual unemployed rate to around 17 percent.

Jobs. The president also stated during his first State of the Union that the administration was on track to create 1.5 million jobs by 2011, using the funds in the bailout or the Recovery Act. In the next breath, he demanded a jobs bill "on his desk without delay." What about the 1.5 million jobs that are on their way? I interpreted this as his counting on someone else to come up with a plan for jobs and just making up a number to appeal to the disturbed public.

Small Business. On the jobs topic, he said he supported small businesses, but where has he demonstrated that? In fact, he was the one who campaigned on not renewing the Bush tax cuts for people who make over $250,000, and mandating that businesses that employ over fifty people provide health care benefits. What encouragement is that for small businesses to expand and succeed? How can people support this hypocrisy?

A further measure of our president's incompetence was displayed during his September address to congress and the nation. He outlined a new bill proposing just shy of five hundred billion dollars of new spending in infrastructure and government programs that is already "paid for" according to him. President Obama also outlined many new tax cuts for small businesses and new incentives for companies that hire in 2012. However, he made no mention of the impact of his health care bill affecting companies that want to expand past forty-nine employees.

> You want to expand the government by *taxing* the people who *hire* the people that pay the taxes so the government can function, right?

As I do agree with many of the cuts he proposed and agree many of them would move us in a productive direction, I do not agree with how he intends to fund them and the rest of his new stimulus ideas. The phrase "their fair share" was thrown out in regard to big corporations and wealthy individuals when it came to their taxes again. Okay, Mr. President, explain this to me again. You want to expand the government by *taxing* the people who *hire* the people that *pay the taxes* so the government can function, right? Call me crazy, but I still don't think you get it, Sir.

Also around the time of his speech, a handful of millionaires and billionaires said they should, in fact, be taxed more because they can afford it. Here is what I say to all those idiotic rich folks out there who agreed with that philosophy: the amount of taxes people pay every year to the federal government is simply the minimum you are required to pay. Nothing is stopping you from paying 40, 50 or even 100 percent of your income back to the government, if you should feel the desire to do so. But just because you want to do that, don't tell other folks what to do with their money.

THE PLOY

Along with this, President Obama illustrated the bipartisan factor of the bill by stating who came up with what parts or ideas in it. This is what makes him such a snake in the grass. He publicly stated all the appealing parts of the bill without uncovering the new regulations and committees that will bicker and waste time and money trying to accomplish all these government-initiated projects and programs. It's all a political ploy while he builds his reelection campaign. What will happen is that once the jobs bill has been fully read and understood, most Republicans will most likely not agree with the stipulations involved with it. While many Republicans probably had input while it was being written, most of those ideas will come with progressive, left-leaning stipulations that negate the very basis of capitalist reasoning. In effect, the majority of Republicans will not vote for it.

This will look good for Obama when it gets to the House of Representatives. The Republicans who don't vote for it will be smeared by the mainstream media as not caring about jobs and other political rhetoric like that. What the public needs to know is that this is just another ploy to expand the government. As I have said before, true economic success is not defined by federally funded infrastructure projects or fancy policies but by motivated, hardworking Americans who are not suppressed by regulations to be able to expand their own businesses.

My suggestion is far from a refined proposal, but it's along these lines: if you start a business, you will be able to apply for a government loan for "x" amount of money based on your success. Measured by a matrix of the number of employees, volume of sales, and overall financial success, you would be responsible to pay back potentially less than your original principal of the loan, because your value and productivity to the economy would be financially more beneficial than repaying the actual loan. Hence, the government has the flexibility to forgive a fraction or the entire principal loan.

Though I know this is not a perfect plan, it is, in fact, another government program and would only work in the short run, but it truly satisfies both parties in the meantime. For the Republicans it will generate more private business, which will in turn generate tax revenue due to the higher number of people actually paying taxes. And it will appease the Democrats because they will get to spend some money, which we know they love to do, and they would get another government program. Of course, they would have to get rid of all the other job panels and things like that.

Despite President Obama's being so adamant about passing the bill immediately, as he clearly stated more than fifteen times during his monologue, many days after, Speaker Boehner still had not received any bill to present to congress. Crazy? Think, *I can go to the Fed-Ex store and have a package shipped over night to LA for less than fifty bucks, and you are telling me that the president of the United States can't get a piece of legislation delivered down the street in a day?* There are two possible explanations for that: (a) the government is really that inefficient, which is very possible, or (2) the bill hadn't, in fact, been written yet, due in part again to the incompetence of the current administration. I personally believe the latter is more likely.

Inexperience Reigns

It was stated that our fearless leader has a plan to double our exports to compete in an international market, and by 2035 to have 80 percent of America running off "clean energy." How are we supposed to do that when you want to seriously over tax our businesses for things like dust and CO_2 emissions? Dumping taxpayer dollars into a system to meet arbitrary numbers is ridiculous.

Do you want to know why we have lost our globally competitive edge? The Chinese can make a pair of shoes for about five cents. How are we supposed to compete with that while paying all these crazy taxes? As for our "green energy," China builds most of the components for that as well. This inexperience is reflected by Obama's cabinet members' business history as well.

On an episode of Glenn Beck's show, he showed a graph that illustrated the percentage of each past president's cabinet who had worked in the private business sector prior to their appointment to the cabinet. The private business sector is real-life business, not a government job. Below is the chart presented by Mr. Beck on his show. Please study it carefully, and I think you'll see where the problem lies.

President	%
T. Roosevelt	38
Taft	40
Wilson	52
Harding	49
Coolidge	48
Hoover	42
F. Roosevelt	50
Truman	50
Eisenhower	57
Kennedy	30
Johnson	47
Nixon	53
Ford	42
Carter	32
Reagan	56
G.H.W. Bush	51
Clinton	39
G.W. Bush	55

And the least experienced award goes to . . .

Obama	8

> He was too busy appointing his homies as czars to realize that no one around him had any experience. Shame on you, America, for voting him into office!

Congratulations, Mr. President, you appointed a bunch of inexperienced idealist idiots. Only 8 percent? He was too busy appointing his homies as czars to realize that no one around him had any experience. You've got to be kidding me. Shame on you, America, for voting him into office! He brings to the table the least business experience by far of the last nineteen presidents. In a time when America needs to be more financially conscious than ever, President Obama seated a bunch of cabinet members with little to no financial experience. These are the people trying to tell big corporations through massive oversight, stipulations, and taxes how to run their businesses? How do they know what's best for GM, Chrysler, and Wall Street? Even after all this, Obama appointed Erskine Bowles to review the financial situation. In July, he came back to the administration and said something to the effect that, "If you don't stop the spending, this country will go broke. You can't tax your way out of it."

I have a common-sense question for you: how can the president of the most powerful nation, the one with the most successful economic system in the history of the world, stand and talk about business when he's never worked for one? It runs parallel to not serving in the military but still being in charge of it, as we discussed earlier. This may explain a lot of the endless spending with no real understanding of the consequences. Any real business executive would realize that, if the first bailout didn't make a difference, subsequent ones probably wouldn't either.

The Recovery Act has many unnecessary projects that really don't contribute anything aside from aiding in spending more money and creating a few *temporary* jobs. In fact, it cost you, the taxpayer, well over $200,000 per job created by the bailout program. I don't make nearly $200,000 a year, so why should it cost that much to create a government job, some of them as simple as shoveling dirt?

An example of one of these projects brought up during Obama's first and second State of the Union speeches was a high-speed railroad. We have some of the best and most available transportation systems in the world already, and you think we need a high-speed train at the expense of the taxpayers? There are many more important issues at hand. Mr. Obama asked anyone with a better idea for spending or fixing the economy to come forward. Perhaps he meant anyone with a better idea that appealed to him, because the GOP has been pushing tactics to his desk that have historically worked for many similar economic problems, and yet none have been implemented.

One of the ideas was to *stop cramming the health care bill down America's throat; we can't fund it*. But that didn't work. Thank God for the ruling of the Florida federal judge on that one. The right has been consistently throwing ideas and tactics at the Obama administration, which are almost always met with a lack of bipartisan enthusiasm. There is a feeling in the majority of the democratic side that you can just spend, spend, spend with no repercussions for the country. I sincerely hope the new Republican House of Representatives just puts a sock in Pelosi's mouth for the rest of her time in office. Why can't these people balance a budget as you and I balance ours?

There were some very clear lines drawn during Obama's first two years that were strongly illustrated during the State of the Union speeches. There seems to be a shared feeling on the left that the Republicans think that if Obama loses then they win. In a way, that is correct, but the only reason that's the case is because Obama stands for everything the Republican Party opposes. If Bush had tried some of the shenanigans that Obama has, the GOP would have opposed him too. It's not that we want Obama to lose; it's that we want this country to win. The president told the Republicans to stop voting against every bill he tried to pass. Perhaps we would if he stopped coming up with ideas and policies that suck.

On both occasions, there was a big emphasis on what is going to be done, but nothing was said about the current state or what has been done. (Does the name "State of the Union" mean anything to you?) This was due in large part to the fact that there had been nothing actually accomplished to date. Groups like the Tea Party, keep up the good work, because we need to do something to redirect this country from becoming the next Communist nation in the history books.

ARIZONA'S LAW

The protest and federal lawsuit over the Arizona immigration law is yet another clown show brought to you by the same morons who were sworn in to uphold the nearly verbatim federal law. In case you live under a rock, Arizona passed a state law that was well within their rights to help stop and regulate the influx of illegal immigrants. In recent years, violence, drugs, and immigrant trafficking have become a plague on the border. Governor Janice K. Brewer, in twelve pages, reinforced federal law by making it state law. While Attorney General Eric Holder and Homeland Security Secretary Janet Napolitano publicly ridiculed it, when confronted on the stand about it, they both admitted that they had not read it prior to their negative comments. That didn't prevent them from making bold statements about how it will lead to racial profiling. In fact, the law strictly prohibits any type of racial profiling and says that law enforcement can under no circumstances arbitrarily inquire solely about a person's citizenship; the person must have committed a crime warranting the proof of identification.

The federal government wasted more taxpayer dollars by filing a lawsuit against the state of Arizona over the law. Really? Where are the priorities? Why would the federal government sue a state for trying to uphold what is already federal law, but not sue or take any action against places like San Francisco for harboring and even protecting these illegals in defiance of federal law? Arizona is trying to seal our borders to protect the country, something that the feds are supposed to do. Why would anyone—Democrat or Republican—dispute that law? Despite the anointed one's promise of sending more national guard troops to the border, which he never delivered, the government has now deemed areas inside our borders unsafe while they continue to dispute the law. My head hurts from trying to understand what is going on in DC.

Wikileaks

Along the lines of fighting for the wrong people's rights is the issue of Wikileaks. Why has someone not taken out Julian Assange or other members of his organization? Moreover, why was there talk of his being nominated for the Nobel Peace Prize? We are overseas killing people for the same root reason—because they have the intent to endanger America. This guy has done more damage than most terrorists that we kill in Iraq or Afghanistan. How about the army private who gave him the information? Is that not treason, punishable by death at a time of war? Why are people around the world rallying for his support and even some saying he is a patriot? The government has a right to keep some things secret, as I have said before; sometimes people just don't have a right to know. I know you progressives don't believe there is any evil in the world aside from Fox News, but there is, and sometimes to deal with it, confidential meetings, phone calls, and policy making need to take place.

The lack of sound leadership and competence from this administration was never so prominent as it was during the 2011 debt-ceiling debates. Speaker Boehner proposed countless scenarios to cut spending and right the deficit. There was not one plan introduced by the Democrats that addressed the nation's biggest problem, spending. All they seem to want to do is spend unconditionally and raise taxes to cover the difference. As I said earlier, president Obama has not only campaigned on "no new taxes," but he clearly stated on many occasions that raising taxes during a recession would be detrimental to the nation's recovery. This sort of incompetence is intolerable.

GULF OIL SPILL

I've tried to save the best example of the administration's ignorance for last. Remember the oil spill in the Gulf? That was the worst man-made disaster in the history of mankind, and it probably will be for the rest of time. How is it that Bush was crucified for an improper, half-baked, and late response to Katrina when he responded in a few days to the disaster, but Obama spent weeks fumbling about, trying to decide whether or not to give federal aid on top of turning down other nations' voluntary, uncompensated assistance, in the cleanup, with very little negative press? That blows my mind—media bias, ya think?

> I honestly lose sleep over how someone so foolish got elected president. While he is still my boss, I hate the way he does—or does not do—his job.

There were millions of gallons of oil spewing into the Gulf every day, threatening our shores and more importantly, our already teetering economy, and these guys would rather file suits about who is responsible than spend the same federal money and time fixing it. We know whose fault it is; British Petroleum (BP) even admitted it and took full responsibility prior to the hearings. So what are you getting at, dude? Get a cap on the thing and then point the finger at whomever you want. You could have blamed me if it just got the cap on faster.

On top of all this, with an already beat-up job market, our presidential masterminds decided that it would be a good idea to halt all offshore drilling.

That cut more jobs and slowed our domestic oil production, two things that we really couldn't afford at the time. I honestly lose sleep over how someone so foolish got elected president. While he is still my boss, I hate the way he does—or more accurately does *not* do—his job.

The Real Questions

Before I finish here, I want to ask you a few questions. Actually go through each one and answer it for yourself. For you Obama supporters out there, when you are finished, really evaluate your views.

1. If George W. Bush had been the first president to need a teleprompter to be able to get through any meeting with the press, would you have laughed?

2. If George W. Bush had spent hundreds of thousands of taxpayer dollars to take Laura Bush to a play in NYC, would you have been angry?

3. If Bill O'Reilly had made a joke at the expense of the Special Olympics, would you have approved?

4. If Ronald Reagan had given the Queen of England an iPod containing videos of his speeches, would you have thought this embarrassingly narcissistic and tacky?

5. If George W. Bush had bowed to the king of Saudi Arabia, would you have approved?

6. If Condoleezza Rice had visited Austria and made reference to the nonexistent "Austrian language," would you have brushed it off as a minor slip?

7. If George W. Bush had filled his cabinet and circle of advisers with people who cannot seem to keep current in their income taxes, would you have approved?

8. If John McCain had been so Spanish illiterate as to refer to "Cinco de Cuatro" in front of the Mexican ambassador when it was the 5th of May (*Cinco de Mayo*), and continued to flub it when he tried again, would you have winced in embarrassment?

9. If Sarah Palin had misspelled the word advice, would you have hammered her for it for years, as Dan Quayle and potato, as proof of what a dunce she is?

10. If George W. Bush had burned nine thousand gallons of jet fuel to go plant a single tree on Earth Day, would you have concluded that he's a hypocrite?

11. If George W. Bush's administration had okayed *Air Force One's* flying low over millions of people in downtown Manhattan, followed by a jet fighter, causing widespread panic, would you have wondered whether he actually gets what happened on 9/11?

12. Or if George W. Bush had failed to send relief aid to flood victims throughout the Midwest, even though more people were killed or made homeless than in New Orleans, would you want it made into a major ongoing political issue with claims of racism and incompetence?

13. If George W. Bush had created the positions of thirty-two czars who report directly to him, bypassing the House and Senate on much of what is happening in America, would you have questioned the administration's takeover of America?

14. If the prime minister of Canada had ordered the firing of the CEO of a major American corporation, though he has about the same authority to do so as Obama, would you consider him a radical?

15. If Henry Paulson, the treasury secretary under Bush, had proposed to double the national debt, which had taken more than two centuries to accumulate, in one year, would you have approved?

16. What if he had then proposed to double the debt again within ten years, would you not have hit the street in protest?

17. What if John McCain had written a book wherein he discusses being mentored as a youth by Frank Marshall Davis, an avowed Communist? Would you have voted him in? Or if he had sought the endorsement of the Marxist Party for his senate seat, would you have approved?

18 If any other president chose not to wear an American flag pin, would you approve?

19. And lastly, if any president had traveled the globe apologizing for America's success, power, and concern for other nations, would you have approved?

So, tell me again, what is it about Obama that makes him so brilliant and impressive? Since he has done all of these things and is still praised as a great leader, you have to ask, "Why?" Can't think of anything? Me neither, but as always, if my facts are wrong, feel free to call me out. Just make sure you have *your* facts together.

ELEVEN

Proposed Solutions

While our society has been moving farther away from what we were intended to be, it's not too late for change, right, Obama? I believe there are many ways to solve the problems of today's high governmental dependency, you-owe-me attitude, loss of touch with our roots, political correctness, and the emasculation of society. Getting away from these ideas would be met with great opposition for the first few years, but once fully integrated into our society, they would generate self-reliance and economic stability in the long run.

The problem is that the government has such a long and steady pattern of "aiding the less fortunate" (I call them bums who don't want to work), that any direction other than giving more handouts and interventions would cause a major drop in political approval. Since that's all most politicians seem to care about, my proposals and other rational true American values would be swept under the rug and never heard on Capitol Hill.

I know you are all anxious to hear how I would solve all the problems I've complained about throughout this book, so here are my ideas.

CUT BACK HANDOUTS

First, we cut back all handouts. Welfare outside of Social Security and aspects of Medicare (which people pay into their whole lives) should be scrutinized. Persons outside of Social Security and Medicare receiving any type of government aid would be drug tested at random; if their tests are positive, there would be an immediate cut of all their benefits, period— no hearing, no reapplying, done! The same goes for anyone committing a crime; it would make them ineligible, forever. The ball is in their court; if they choose to live outside the law, they will be choosing to live without the system. No person would be permitted to receive more than one year of combined time on any government aid in his or her lifetime.

> If you don't have a job, get one. If you can't find one, invent one. This country was founded on the mortar of entrepreneurism.

If you don't have a job, get one. If you can't find one, invent one. This country was founded on the mortar of entrepreneurism. The immediate consequences of this plan could unfortunately lead to suffering, but necessity breeds motivation. This is where good-hearted charity would come in. Charity tends to help people who cannot help themselves, not those who won't help themselves. By these means, the system would assume more accountability.

BORDER PROTECTION

The federal government would protect our borders. There would be fences (well into the American side) with signs stating that, if you cross this fence, you will be shot, until dead. No questions asked. If a person sees a fence in the vicinity of a national border and decides to scale and cross it, he knows what he is doing. If he doesn't, the world is a better place without him anyway. Why would people put up a fence if they didn't want to keep other people out?

Going along with that, the ten to twelve million illegal aliens now in the US would be sought out. They would be given two options:

(1) purchase and obtain citizenship only if they can prove they have been here for more than two years. The buy-in could be set at maybe $10,000 and, until paid off, the immigrants would maintain a status much like someone on probation. Any crime, failure of random drug test, avoidable loss of job, or anything not in keeping with good citizenship would forfeit their money and would result in immediate deportation. In addition to that, if they committed any crime during their first five years in the country, then it would result in immediate deportation and forfeiture of all assets. Also, as an immigrant, if they were more than thirty years of age at the time of immigration, they would not be eligible for Social Security or Medicare. Immigrants would also never be entitled to welfare or unemployment benefits.

(2) Option two would be, well, take a hike. There would be no free amnesty. Imagine if we charged each illegal immigrant $10,000 dollars, and there are well over 12 million living here today, that would total over 100 billion dollars in revenue for the government. And if they couldn't pay, deport them. Bam! Put me in for the Pulitzer Prize, baby.

To accomplish this, every transaction—whether cash, check, or charge— in America would, for two years, require you to produce a government-issued ID. It could be a passport, visa, or something else that denotes some sort of accountability to American logistics. Companies and businesses not adhering to these laws would have all assets seized and used to fund our border security and reduce our national deficit. Some would still slip through the cracks, but many would be caught. Mexico would be held accountable for its criminal citizens here in America who need deportation or are processed through our justice system.

OUR LAWS

The problem with society today is there are too many gray areas in laws and standards. Basing laws on right and wrong, instead of on political correctness, would eliminate these. Laws would be simplified and broken down to explain their actual intent. Instead of making more laws or complicating vernacular to aid in altered interpretations, we would simply enforce the laws we already have, such as gun laws. Racial or personal profiling would be procedural, and if the person who was profiled turns out to be a law-abiding citizen, it would not be acceptable for them to file charges or initiate a public outcry about their rights being violated. Things like criminals getting off the hook because the evidence was not acquired legally would go away. If there were evidence that someone committed a crime, no matter how it was acquired, it would be valid. However, if the person who acquired it did so illegally, then he or she would be charged accordingly.

> The problem with society today is there are too many gray areas in laws and standards. Basing laws on right and wrong, instead of political correctness, would eliminate these.

PRISONS

Our prisons for convicted criminals would be much harsher than they are today. If you kill, you would be killed. Child molesters and other assaults on minors would be tried with the same severity as murderers. Much as they do now, crimes would be classified according to severity, but there would be no plea-bargaining to lesser charges for committing a crime. Just enough food would be provided to keep the prisoner alive, blankets and comfort items would be minimal, and if inmates decided to have a fight in prison, let them fight, and afterward punish them appropriately. The punishment should not only fit the crime, but it should be tenfold. That criminal broke the laws of society, visited wrongdoing on an innocent person or people against their will, and now that victim has to live with that for the rest of his or her life—why should the criminal not pay a more severe punishment?

WARS

Wars would be fought to win. There would need to be a definition of victory prior to engaging, not just "stability of the region." People and countries are either with us or against us, and if you are not part of the solution, then you are part of the problem. Host nations, such as Iraq and Afghanistan, would be held accountable for terrorists dwelling and training in their nations. Wars would be waged against the country or host nation of the enemy for not attending to the issues that caused harm to America, unless they were already legitimately engaged in a solution, at which point we would offer our assistance under our terms. The elected officials of these countries so often fund and support our opposition behind closed doors; if they were held accountable for terrorist actions, they would not only stop supporting them, but I'm pretty sure they would try to fix the problem themselves, if they knew they were being targeted by American forces. This would motivate them more than negotiations or sanctions would. If a country needs financial or military assistance or aid, then repayment would be negotiated prior to action. Every country has something to offer, so there need be no free rides. We are a superpower whether we like it or not, right, Mr. President? Let's start acting like one, rather than like a babysitter with an ATM card.

POLITICIANS

Politicians would be held to campaign promises or removed from office. Too often, people vote for someone based on his or her campaign promises, and as soon as elected, the politician turns to a completely different agenda. Major political decisions and bills would be put to a vote of Congress, Senate, the president, and the public, requiring a three-party majority to pass something, such as this health care bill, before it could become law. All the facts would be presented to the public; yes, that's right, all two thousand pages in the health care law, for instance, and politicians would have a chance to vote on them and fine-tune the details only after they read the whole bill.

Once a year, the public would have the right to vote any representative in office, including the president, out of their position by a 66 percent majority of the counted votes, at which point the next-in-line would take over until the next scheduled election. Every man would be required to serve two years in the military or civil service, and anyone running for office would have to have served the same, male or female. This would provide a strong basis for a self-reliant and independent citizenry.

VOTING

In light of that, there would be a test in order to vote. It would be much like an American citizenship test. It would contain things like American history, such as, "Name the last five presidents," or "Who was the president during the Civil War?" It would also contain basic financial questions, such as, "If you spend ten dollars and take in eight, do you have a deficit or a surplus?" and other questions relevant to the American way. You would have to test at the voting station where you vote immediately prior to casting your vote. Tests like this would prevent idiots from voting and help avoid situations like what happened in the 2010 state senate election in the Los Angeles district in California.

Jenny Oropeza was reelected, despite the fact that she had been dead for over two weeks. And lastly, if you have a criminal record, you would not be allowed to vote, let alone hold a seat in a federal office.

THE CONSTITUTION

Our Constitution and its values would be the highest of legal documents and procedures, and it would be honored as such. Laws, fees, taxes, and stipulations could not be imposed to limit it, and any attempt would be treated as criminal. When Adam Sharp of the St. Louis Tea Party asked Rep. Phil Hare which part of the Constitution authorizes the government to mandate that all Americans buy a private product, such as health insurance, the Illinois Democrat replied, "I don't worry about the Constitution on this." What? Are you serious? This guy should have lost his job and gone to jail for treason. If Republicans said that, they would be crucified.

The Pledge of Allegiance would be encouraged in schools, and the morals of our founding Judeo-Christian religion would be taught as part of the history curriculum, not abolished from education. No one would be forced to practice any religion, but nevertheless it would be explained as our foundation.

MILITARY PERFORMANCE

All people have the right of free speech, and this includes military personnel. If their superior were wrong or not fit for the job, then they would have the right to state their case and say so without consequences, while still adhering to military standard. Military promotions would not be based on a written test, as they currently are in the navy. There would be three criteria: physical fitness, peer evaluations, and performance. Once rank was made, demotions would be in order for those not holding to standard in all categories. In the military, unions, or any other bureaucracy, the decision to fire a subordinate would be made by the immediate superior, with appeal possible only to one level higher. If fired, the person's paycheck would stop that day, and they would not be moved to another department. This would solve the problem of someone who doesn't even know the individual having to make the decision to can them.

GUNS

Every law-abiding citizen would have the right to carry a gun, no matter where you live. The carry permit would be federal and not state based, and firearms would not be taxed to make them unaffordable. If you don't like guns, then don't buy them. But don't tell others they can't have theirs. Hold people accountable under our current laws for firearms, and there will be little to worry about. Think about when the Florida school board gunman Clay Duke held all the men at gunpoint over the firing of his wife. Imagine if some members in the room had been allowed to carry a gun then. It would not have gone on even half as long as it did. How about the Columbine High School incident or the Virginia Tech shooting or the Arizona shooting? The criminals will get guns no matter what. But making it easier for law-abiding citizens to defend themselves against those criminals will make America safer.

PROPOSED SOLUTIONS

AFFIRMATIVE ACTION

Affirmative action would go away. If you get the score, you get the job. There would be no more need for mandating a racially diverse force. Black rights and other racial support groups would dwindle and fade, because they would no longer be needed, because there would be true equal opportunity. These organizations only further the boundaries of racism and create animosity between races. People who argue otherwise are, in essence, racists. Al Sharpton and people like him, who believe their race deserves considerations that others don't, would be discredited.

Organizations like the ACLU and NAMBLA would be shut down and prosecuted for aiding and supporting cases of child molesters, terrorists, and other criminals. Because we all have equal rights and opportunities, there would be no need for these human rights protesters. When a white kid beats up a black kid, race would be left out of it completely, and they would be tried on facts alone. If someone is racist, fine; it is his or her right, and it is your right to disagree with it.

GOVERNMENT

Last, but certainly not least, Government, get your big, greedy hands out of my pockets. The less you are in the picture, the better. Society will right itself out of necessity. By intervening, you are building up the companies and organizations that simple economics has deemed unfit to survive, just like Obama's foolproof investment, Solyndra. Don't make more laws and regulations. Focus on running the country, and let Americans focus on their lives and bank accounts, instead of how to survive while filling yours. Finally, don't spend money you don't have. Guess what? If you have to raise the retirement age to seventy, so be it. In the interest of a balanced budget and my future children not suffering, I would be happy to work the extra five years.

Maybe making Congress's retirement and benefits plan the same as everyone else's might get us on the right track.

Speaking of the right track, we don't need a high-speed railroad or any other shovel-ready government jobs for that matter. We need more Americans to employ Americans, and that can only happen by, you guessed it, less government oversight. "By the people, for the people," because we the people make up America, and that is what we are trying to save.

BEFORE IT'S TOO LATE

Some of these may seem like extreme proposals, but unfortunately we are presented with extreme circumstances these days. Inevitably, if you want to change something, it will be watered down and compromised before it gets passed or enforced. These are what I believe would get this country back on the right track. As I have said before, I'm not always right, and I don't know everything by a long shot, but something profound needs to be done, and soon. America, you have the power to fix this and ensure that it will never happen again.

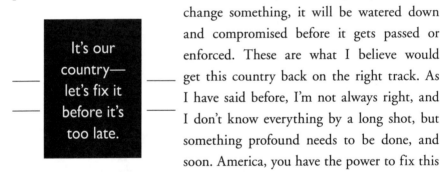

It's our country—let's fix it before it's too late.

Please, stand up for what is right, even when no one is looking. Vote. And, most of all, be personally responsible. It's our country—let's fix it before it's too late.

Born in 1983, I am too young and inexperienced to throw my hat in the ring for any elections now, but rest assured, I intend to fix this country one way or another before my life is over.

God bless America!

NOTES

CHAPTER TWO

1. Jefferson, Thomas. Library of Congress, "Jefferson's Letter to the Danbury Baptists." Accessed December 13, 2011 http://www.loc.gov/lcib/9806/danpre.html
2. Ronald Reagan. BrainyQuote.com, Xplore Inc., 2011. Accessed December 13, 2011. http://www.brainyquote.com/quotes/quotes/r/ronaldreag385754.html.
3. *U.S. Constitution.* Art. II, Sec. 2.
4. *U.S. Constitution.* Art. II, Sec. 4.
5. *U.S. Constitution.* Art. III, Sec.3.
6. *U.S. Constitution,* Art.XI.
7. *U.S. Constitution,* Amend.I.
8. *U.S. Constitution.* Amend.II.
9. Kloos, Marko. The Munchkin Wrangler, "Why the Gun is Civilization." Accessed December 13, 2011. http://munchkinwrangler.wordpress.com/2007/03/23/why-the-gun-is-civilization/.
10. Associated Press, "Grand jury indicts Soles in shooting." Accessed December 19, 2011. http://www.wral.com/news/state/story/6757337/.
11. *U.S. Constitution.* Amend.IV.

CHAPTER FOUR

1. Associated Press, "Supreme Court to Hear White Firefighters' Case on Affirmative Action." Accessed December 13, 2011. http://www.foxnews.com/story/0,2933,517448,00.html.
2. Jessup, Meredith. The Blaze, "Guess How Many People Feel Al Sharpton is a Pinhead . . ." Accessed December 19, 2011. http://www.theblaze.com/stories/guess-how-many-people-feel-al-sharpton-is-a-pinhead/.
3. HarpWeek, LLC, "Denis Kearney and the California Anti-Chinese Campaign." Accessed December 13, 2011. http://immigrants.harpweek.com/ChineseAmericans/2KeyIssues/DenisKearneyCalifAnti.htm.

4. Associated Press, "Harry Reid 'Negro' Comment: Reid Apologizes for 'No Negro Dialect' Comment." Accessed December 19, 2011. http://www. huffingtonpost.com/2010/01/09/harry-reid-negro-comment-_n_417406.html.
5. Fox News, "New Black Panther Leader Defends Group in Voter Intimidation Case." Accessed December 19, 2011. http://www.foxnews. com/politics/2010/07/09/new-black-panther-leader-defends-group-voter-intimidateion-case/.
6. Williams, Juan. Fox News, "Juan Williams: I Was Fired for Telling the Truth." Accessed December 19, 2011. http://www.foxnews.com/opinion/2010/10/21/ juan-williams-npr-fired-trugh-muslim-garb-airplane-oreilley-ellen-weiss-bush/.
7. Fox News, "Senate Report: Ft. Hood Shooting Could've Been Prevented." Accessed December 19, 2011. http://nation.foxnews.com/ft-hood-shooting/2011/02/03/senate-report-ft-hood-shooting-could-ve-been-prevented.
8. Thomas, Devon. CBS News, "Bill O'Reilly On "The View": "Muslims Killed Us on 9/11" [VIDEO]; Co-Hosts Walk Off." Accessed December 19, 2011. http://www.cbsnews.com/8301-31749_162-20019660-10391698.html.
9. Fox News, "Herman Cain Upsets Gov. Rick Perry to Win Florida GOP Straw Poll." Accessed December 19, 2011. http://www.foxnews.com/ politics/2011/09/24/perry-says-rivals-made-mistake-by-skipping-florida-test-vote/.

CHAPTER FIVE

1. Unforgottenangels, "A Child Is Raped for 4 Years And The Judge Sentences the Perp to 60 DAYS in Vermont!" Accessed December 19, 2011. http:// unforgottenangels.wordpress.com/2011/01/30/a-child-is-raped-for-4-years-and-the-judge-sentences-the-perp-to-60-days-in-vermont/.
2. Frick, Ali. Think Progress, "Rohrbacher: Torture At Guantanamo Sikmply 'Hazing Pranks From Some Fraternity.'" Accessed December 19, 2011. http:// thinkprogress.org/politics/2008/06/04-24222/rohrabacher-torture./
3. Spiegel Online, "Interview with Homeland Security Secretary Janet Napolitano 'Away From the Politics of Fear'." Accessed December 19, 2011. http://www. spiegel.de/international/world/0,1518,613330, 00.html.
4. Hill, D.S. News Flavor, "Warning: Right-Wing Extremists are About to Takeover." Accessed December 19, 2011. http://newsflavor.com/opinions/ warning-right-wing-extremists-are-about-to-takeover/.
5. Associated Press, "Pelosi: Lawmakers Should Sacrifice Jobs for Health Care."

Accessed December 19, 2011. http://www.foxnews.com/politics/2010/02/28/pelosi-lawmakers-sacrifice-jobs-health-care/.

6. Hoft, Jim. Gateway Pundit, "Paul McCarney Bashes Bush at White House: "It's Great to Have a President Who Knows What a Library Is" (Video)." Accessed December 19, 2011. http://www.thegatewaypundit.com/2010/06/paul-mccarney-bashes-bush-at-white-house-its-great-to-have-a-resident-who-knows-what-a-library-is/.

7. Cohen, Richard. Washington Post, "George W. Bush as an Avid Reader." Accessed December 19, 2011. http://www.washingtonpost.com/wp-dyn-content/article/2008/12/29/AR2008122901896.html.

8. Blumer, Tom. News Busters, "Blatant vs. Balanced: CNN, MSNBC Played Faves With Mass. Electrion Night Speeches; Fox Carried All of Both." Accessed December 19, 2011. http://newsbusters.org/blogs/tom-blumer/2010/01/25/blatant-vs-balanced-cnn-msnbc-played-faves-mass-electrion-night-speeches-.

9. Gore, Al. EcoMall, "An Inconvenient Truth." Accessed December 19, 2011. http://www.ecomall.com/greenshopping/algorebook.htm.

10. Capitol Hill Blue, "Obama's plan: Undermine, discredit all critics." Accessed December 19, 2011. http://www.capitolhillblue.com/node/20057.

11. Listi, Tony. Conservative Colloquium, "Woodrow Wilson: America's Worst and First Fascist Presicent." Accessed December 19, 2011. http://conservativecolloquium.wordpress.com/2008/05/29/woodrow-wilson-americas-worst-and-first-fascist-president/.

12. McCullagh, Declan. CNet, "Bill would give president emergency control of Internet." Accessed December 19, 2011. http://news.enet.com/8301-13578_3-10320096-18.html.

13. Fox News, "Obama Swipes at Media, Says, 'Information' Onslaught Pressuring 'Democracy'." Accessed December 19, 2011. http://www.foxnews.com/politics/2010/05/11/obama-swipes-media-questions-accuracy-content-environment/.

14. Barr, Andy. Politico, "Joe Klein: Yes, Sarah Palin and Glenn Beck 'seditious'." Accessed December 19, 2011. http://www.politico.com/news/stories/0410/36020.html.

15. Fox News, "Entire Taj Mahal Hotel Reportedly Booked for Obama Mumbai Visit." Accessed December 19, 2011. http://www.foxnews.com/politics/1010/10/24/entire-taj-mahal-hotel-reportedly-booked-obama-mumbai-visit/.

NOTES

CHAPTER SIX

1. Schweikart, Larry. Glenn Beck, "America." Accessed December 19, 2011. http://www.glennbeck.com/content/articles/article/198/36839/.
2. Bureau of Labor Statistics, "Employment Situation Summary." December 19, 2011. http://www.bls.gov/news.release/empsit.nr0.htm.
3. Dinan, Stephen. The Washington Times, "How Bad it Almost Was." Accessed December 19, 2011. http://www.washingtontimes.com/blog/inside-politics/2011/jan/19/how-bad-it-almost-was/.
4. Fox News, "Judge Rules Health Care Law is Unconstitutional." December 19, 2011. http://www.foxnew.com/politics/2011/01/31/judges-ruling-health-care-lawsuit-shift-momentum-coverage-debate/.
5. pg 93letter from Dr. Roger Starner Jones needs to be attrituted to Clarion Ledger in the lead in paragraph not facebook.

CHAPTER SEVEN

1. Fox News, "Culture War Over Boulder High School Panel That Encouraged Students to Have Sex, Break the Law." Accessed December 19, 2011. http://www.foxnews.com/story/0,2933,282334,00.html.
2. The Huffington Post, "Charlie Rangel Scandal." Accessed December 19, 2011. http://www.huffingtonpost.com/2010/11/19/charlie-rangel-scandal-co_n_785879.html.
3. Fox News, "O'Reilly on Troubling Corruption Surrounding Obama." Accessed December 19, 2011. http://www.dailymotion.com/video/x7oymt_fox-news-o-reilly-on-troubling-corr_news.
4. Scared Monkeys, "Barack Obama's 20 Year Pastor & Mentor: Rev. Wright Tells Church Youth All Whites Are Liars." Accessed December 19, 2011. http://scaredmonkeys.com/2011/07/03/barack-obama%E2%80%99s-20-year-pastor-mentor-rev-wright-tells-church-youth-all-whites-are-liars/.
5. Kish, Daniel. US News, "Obama Anti-Coal Energy Agenda Would Hurt America." Accessed December 19, 2011. http://www.usnews.com/opinion/blogs/energy-intelligence/2011/07/20/obama-anti-coal-energy-agenda-would-hurt-america.
6. Torrellas, Rebecca. E&P, "Offshore drilling moratorium affects everyone." Accessed December 19, 2011. http://www.epmag.com/2010/July/item63533.php.
7. Cox, Chris. The Daily Caller, "Obama Campaign Organizing Against Gun

Owners." Accessed December 19, 2011. http://dailycaller.com/2011/09/22/
obama-campaign-organizing-against-gun-owners/.

CHAPTER EIGHT

1. Leonard, Tom. The Telegraph, "US Soldier Shoots Dead Five Comrades in
   Baghdad Stress Clinic." Accessed December 19, 2011. http://www.telegraph.
   co.uk/news/worldnews/middleeast/iraq/5309554/US-soldier-shoots-dead-five-
   comrades-in-Baghdad-stress-clinic.html.

CHAPTER NINE

1. Saad, Lydia. Gallup, "US Debt Ceiling Increase Remains Unpopular
   with Americans." Accessed December 19, 2011. http://www.gallup.com/
   poll/148454/debt-ceiling-increase-remains-unpopular-americans.aspx.
2. Morrissey, Ed. Hot Air, " Obama Speech: Lots of Words, No Solutions."
   Accessed December 19, 2011. http://hotair.com/archives/2011/07/26/obama-
   speech-lots-of-words-no-solutions/.
3. Twilight's Last Gleaming, "The Left's Worst Nightmare: The Truth." Accessed
   December 19, 2011. http://www.twilightslastgleaming.com/they-said-it.htm.
4. Fox News, "Five People Killed During Protests in Egypt." Accessed December
   19, 2011. http://www.foxnews.com/world/2011/01/28/violent-clashes-police-
   break-cairo/.
5. Fox News, "London Students Protest Over Fees." Accessed December 19, 2011.
   http://www.foxnews.com/world/2011/11/09/london-student-protest-over-fees-
   draws-thousands/.
6. Hunter, Chase Kyla. Alternative News Report, "World Financial Markets
   Destabilizing." Accessed December 19, 2011. http://alternativenewsreport.net/
   category/world-financial-markets-destabilizing/.
7. Curwick, Stephen. The University of Washington, "War and Red Scare 1940-
   1960." Accessed December 19, 2011. http://depts.washington.edu/labhist/
   cpproject/curwick.shtml.
8. Time, "Why Obama loves Regan." Accessed December 19, 2011. http://www.
   time.com/time/covers/0,16641,20110207,00.html.
9. Sanders, Richard. "Regime Change: How the CIA put Saddam's Party
   in Power." Accessed December 19, 2011. http://www.hartford-hwp.com/
   archives/51/217.html.

10. Caulfield, Philip. NY Daily News, "Osama Bin Laden's Lair in Abbottabad, Military Town North of Islamabad Served as Terror Hideout." Accessed December 19, 2011. http://articles.nydailynews.com/2011-05-02/news/29521402_1_compound-pakistani-city-military-town.

CHAPTER TEN

1. Strom, Stephanie. NY Times, "On Obama, Acorn and Voter Registration." Accessed December 19, 2011. http://www.nytimes.com/2008/10/11/us/politics/11acorn.html.
2. Woman, Uppity. No Quarter, "ACORN Nailed Registering Dead People in Indiana." Accessed December 19, 2011. http://www.noquarterusa.net/blog/5211/acorn-nailed-registering-dead-people-in-indiana/.
3. Alexander, Rachel. The Free Republic, "Fifty Percent Welfare Nation." Accessed December 19, 2011. http://freerepublic.com/focus/f-news/2805949/posts.
4. MacIntosh, Jeane. NY Post, "1 Voter, 72 Registrations." Accessed December 19, 2011. http://www.nypost.com/p/news/politics/item_8dh7PaKRiPc0BFNPZVnGMM.
5. BreitBart TV, "'Howard Stern Show' Quizzes Obama Supporters in Harlem on Candidate Policies." Accessed December 23, 2011. http://tv.breitbart.com/howard-stern-show-interviews-confused-obama-supporters-in-harlem/.
6. St. Petersburg Times, "No family making less than $250,000 will see "any form of tax increase." Accessed December 23, 2011. http://www.politifact.com/truth-o-meter/promises/obameter/promise/515/no-family-making-less-250000-will-see-any-form-tax/.
7. Reid, Chip. CBS News, "Obama Reneges on Health Care Transparency." Accessed December 23, 2011. http://www.cbsnews.com/stories/2010/01/06/eveningnews/main6064298.shtml.
8. O'Reilly, Bill. Fox News, "Jobs Vs. Debt." Accessed December 23, 2011. http://www.foxnews.com/on-air/oreilly/2011/10/07/bill-oreilly-jobs-vs-debt.
9. Powers, Doug. Associated Press, "Obama to Skip Wreath Laying Ceremony at Arlington on Monday." Accessed December 23, 2011. http://michellemalkin.com/2010/05/25/ap-obama-to-skip-arlington-memorial/.
10. York, Byron. The Washington Examiner, "Disaster Poll: Nearly 70 Percent say dump Dems' Health Care Bill." Accessed December 23, 2011. http://washingtonexaminer.com/blogs/beltway-confidential/disaster-poll-nearly-70-percent-say-dump-dems039-health-care-bill.

11. The Huffington Post, "Barack Obama Golf Trips Already Out Number Bush's." Accessed December 23, 2011. http://www.huffingtonpost.com/2010/04/24/barack-obama-golf-trips-a_n_550635.html
12. Werthmann, Kitty. "America Truly is the Greatest Country in the World. Don't Let Freedom Slip Away." Pg 129-130 WAITING FOR PERMISSION
13. Fox News, "Obama Swipes at Media, Says 'Information' Onslaught Pressuring 'Democracy'." Accessed December 23, 2011. http://www.foxnews.com/politics/2010/05/11/obama-swipes-media-questions-accuracy-content-environment/.
14. Koch, Wendy. USA Today, "How Green is Al Gore's $9 Million Mantecito Oceanfront Villa?" Accessed December 23, 2011. http://content.usatoday.com/communities/greenhouse/post/2010/05/how-green-is-al-gores-9-million-montecito-ocean-front-villa/1.
15. CNN, "Obama Signs Repeal of 'Don't Ask, Don't Tell' Policy." Accessed December 23, 2011. http://articles.cnn.com/2010-12-22/politics/dadt.repeal_1_repeal-openly-gay-men-president-barack-obama?_s=PM:POLITICS.
16. The Huffington Post, "State of the Union Address 2011: Supreme Court Justices Won't All Attend." Accessed December 23, 2011. http://www.huffingtonpost.com/2011/01/25/state-of-the-union-addres_1_n_813663.html
17. Beck, Glenn. "Obama's Speding Freeze is Nothing But Nonsense." Accessed December 23, 2011. http://www.glennbeck.com/content/articles/article/198/35609/.
18. Keegan, Dennis and David West. Remove Them All - Vote 2010, "The Meltdown Simplified." Accessed December 23, 2011. http://www.removethemall.us/what_caused_recession.htm. Pg. 141 end of block quotes WAITING FOR PERMISSION
19. Condon, Stephen. CBS News, "Obama Hails Auto Bailout, Trade Deal in Michigan." Accessed December 23, 2011. http://www.cbsnews.com/8301-503544_162-20120686-503544.html.
20. Cornwall, Jeffrey. The Christian Science Monitor, "The Real Unemployment Rate and Europe's Underground Economy." Accessed December 23, 2011. http://www.csmonitor.com/Business/The-Entrepreneurial-Mind/2011/1109/The-real-unemployment-rate-and-Europe-s-underground-economy.
21. Perge, Damir. Entrepreneurdex, "Statdex: % of President's Cabinet Members with Business Experience." Accessed December 23, 2011. http://www.entrepreneurdex.com/profiles/blogs/statdex-of-presidents.
22. O'Reilly, Bill. Fox News, "Economic Disaster on the Horizon." Accessed December 23, 2011. http://www.foxnews.com/on-air/oreilly/transcript/economic-disaster-horizon.

23. Media Matters For America, "Doocy Revives "Bogus" Cost-per-Job Math to Attack Stimulus." Accessed December 23, 2011. http://mediamatters.org/research/201108050016.
24. Fox News, "Justice Department Files Suit Against Arizona Immigration Law." Accessed December 23, 2011. http://www.foxnews.com/politics/2010/07/06/justice-department-file-suit-arizona-early-tuesday/.
25. Fox News, "Napolitano Admits She Hasn't Read ArizonaImmigration Law in 'Detail'." Accessed December 23, 2011. http://www.foxnews.com/politics/2010/05/18/napolitano-admits-read-arizona-im

ABOUT THE AUTHOR

The terrorism of 9/11 served as a ferocious wake-up call for Carl Higbie. After graduating from high school in 2002, he spent a couple of years in college all the while thinking about this nation and what he could do to contribute to it. Carl knew that he not only wanted to serve his country, but more than that, he wanted to be a Navy SEAL.

As Carl puts it, he was a mediocre student and a star wrestler in high school. When he decided to go into the navy, Carl encountered nothing but discouragement from those in the recruiting office as well as others along the way. As is characteristic of Carl, he did not let the negativism of others stand in his way, and ultimately he was admitted into the SEAL training team.

Carl has served two deployments to combat areas in the Middle East, and additionally has served in numerous assignments in other parts of the world. He now serves as a SEAL instructor. In his off hours he owns Tarzan Tree Service in Virginia Beach.